Alicia — You are an "Angel"! Love

IMMORTAL ANGEL

A Guardians of Dacia Novel

LONI LYNNE

Believe in Fate!

Loni Lynne

Immortal Angel

Cover Design: Jenji
Cover Photograph: DepositPhotos.com
Editor: Judy Roth
Formatting by: Anessa Books

Spiridus Publishing, Publisher

First Edition: May 2015

DEDICATION

To all the men and women who ever served our great country. For your sacrifices and your dedication. Let us always remember that our freedom is never free.

AUTHOR'S NOTE

The Guardians of Dacia Series

Romania has been called the mystical land of paranormal beings and creatures of the night. Before the Romans conquered their land, Dacia was a mystical land of magic and folk-lore until one man and his army destroyed the closely woven fabric set by the gods between man and beast. Now, cursed by their gods over two thousand years ago, one immortal clan struggles to maintain their private world while still learning to live and protect their human brethren astheir enemy seeks power to destroy the new world.

As the immortals face extinction, a new generation of Dacian blood emerges to unite the clans once more. The world as they know it may never be the same.

If you would like to read more about Tina and Mike's relationship, before ***Immortal Angel****, please read the novella,* ***Immortal Wounds*** *available as eBook and print from your fine book distributors. It is not mandetory, as the book stands alone, but it does give you more insight into their past.*

Immortal Angel

Tina Johnston is left heartbroken afterthe man she loves, turns her away. She's too young and naïve to be able to understand the immortal, Vietnam warrior who suffers from the nightmare of his past. So she decides to work for the Delvante Clan and train to be an assistant to the immortal Dacians. What she doesn't know is that her first assignment is about to take her into a world of danger and action, in which the very people she's learning to protect are out to hunt her down and make her one of their own.

Vietnam was forty years ago yet Mike Linder can't forget the horrors of the past. His struggle with PTSD has no place for the lovely Tina Johnston. As much as he wants her out of his life, he can't bear to be without her. What they shared the past few months is beyond anything he deserves. But when he finds she's gone to work for his boss, Rick Delvante and is sent to infiltrate a group of rogue vampires in Germany, he is beside himself. The only thing he can do is face his worst fear and go into battle once more to bring her home safely.

But what he finds is not the woman he left behind. Is he too late to save his Immortal Angel?

CHAPTER ONE

APRIL—

Tina Johnston pressed the doorbell and its peal echoed within the ranch-style log cabin. The darkened woods at night surrounded her with its loneliness and mystery, but it was part of its charm. She missed the solitude and being with Mike Linder out here in the middle of nowhere. In a few short months, they'd made so many happy memories. A lifetime of happiness...until...

The security camera above the door swiveled with a slight electronic buzz. He was home! She waved, holding up the plain brown paper bag tied with blue and gold ribbon she'd curled and decorated herself.

Impatiently, she waited. It would take him a while to trek up to the "house" part of his domain. The log cabin rancher wasa façade for his actual cavernous abode secluded beneath the building, protecting who and what he was. Protective glass and rock walls sheltered him from the harmful rays of sunlight and mortals who might destroy him because of his lifestyle.

Moments went by. She rang the doorbell again. The camera didn't move this time. Her heart slumped. Was he avoiding her? She'd tried to call, text, email but to no avail. Mike had blocked her from his phone. This birthday gift was a last ditch effort to try and get back into his life. He'd been unreasonable. He didn't think she could handle their relationship.

Not wanting to give up on their future, she thought about ringing the doorbell again when the heavy wooden door opened to reveal a disheveled, shirtless Mike Linder. His sexy shadow of scruff and mussed, short blond hair were forever etched in her heart. Tina loved seeing him after they'd...

"What's up?" he asked gruffly.

Her heart bottomed out at the thought. His faded, unbuttoned jeans teased a narrow strip of hair that lead to—

"I...I thought...I mean I wanted to stop by and say happy birthday. I brought you a gift."

"That's thoughtful of you, Tina. Thank you."

"It's just a little something. I didn't know what to get you. I hope you like it though." She handed it to him with trembling fingers.

An awkward moment of silence stretched endlessly as Mike raked his fingers through his hair. "I'd invite you inside but...I... um have company."

She grimaced. He'd already replaced her with someone else. Fighting off the lump in her throat that threatened to break through on a sob, she smiled and nodded as if his statement hadn't cleaved her heart in two.

Unable to bear the heartache of knowing he'd taken pleasure in another woman's body, she turned away, nearly running to her car. Away from the pain. She knew what she had to do now.

* * *

Mike watched the retreating taillights of Tina's car as long as he could. Well, that was that. The final straw. Leaning against the door jamb he gathered his wits as the taste of her sweet lips lingered like a sip of cool, fresh water. He'd thirsted for her for so long. But now? She wouldn't be back again.

It's for the best, man. You are not what she needs.

Padding barefoot back down into his solitary domain of rock and tinted security glass, he dropped onto the leather sectional, placing the birthday present on the coffee table in front of him. He glared at the bag as if it contained C4. Emotionally, it just might.

Cursing himself for being a coward, he went to pour himself a glass of synthetic hemoglobin, adding a shot of whiskey for good measure. The mirrored insert near his bar reflected a man in his prime...twenty-seven years old...again.

He hadn't aged since 1969. Forty-five years of immortality kept a man looking young and virile. But the tortured soul of a seventy-two year old Vietnam veteran outweighed the youthful vitality.

"Well, you've done it old man. You've managed to send the one woman who accepts you for what you are, running." He toasted his reflection in the glass and gulped down a healthy sip, painfully forcing it past the lump in his throat.

He didn't have any "company,"but he'd figured it might be the only way to get her to understand he was an asshole and she didn't need him in her life. What better way than have her assume he'd moved on and had someone else in his bed. She'd forget about him eventually, marry someone more deserving and normal, have children...

Fuck.

The thought of another man touching her, tasting her sweetness, hearing her laughter, making her smile, much less giving her a child had his teeth on edge. He had no one else to blame though. He'd done it to himself.

The gift beckoned to him like a beacon in a dark storm. The simple brown bag, its hemp handles decorated with metallic blue and gold curled ribbon...Navy colors. Intrigue drew him. What could Tina have bought that would rival the happiness she'd given him? He'd loved listening to her ideas and dreams. She was intelligent and intellectual. Someone he could have a true conversation with. He'd found her fascinating. So it would only go to show the gift would equal her inspirational ideals.

Just open the damn thing. Or are you a chicken-shit?

There were days he wished he could punch his conscience in the face. Nothing like having your inner-self fuck with your emotions.

Walking back over to the couch he sat in front of the gift bag, examining it. He wasn't defusing a bomb, it was a simple gift. But his palms didn't know the difference, damp as they were.

With a delicacy he did not possess, he untied the ribbon and opened the bag. A heavy cardboard box nestled among strips of blue and gold paper greeted him along with a card. Lifting the box out and placing it on the table, he removed the tiny pieces of tape and opened the box lid.

A glass globe. A glass water globe wrapped in tissue paper. Pulling the item out all the way, it tinkled with music. He knew the song. The Navy Hymn. Tina must have wound it so that it would play automatically.

He shook the globe and sparkling snow fell around the tiny

sculpture of the United States Naval Academy Chapel lit up with tiny painted lights. In front of the chapel a horse drawn carriage carried a man dressed in Navy blues with a woman in a warm coat and fur muff sitting beside him.

His nostrils flared with a tingling sensation that set off a sting in his eyes. His throat tightened, his fingers clenched into fists. Setting the globe down carefully, Mike stared at it as if it *were* a ticking time bomb. In reality, it was worse. A bomb killed instantly, this pierced his soul like a barb that couldn't be drawn. It would fester and bleed for the rest of his eternity. Being immortal, that would be a helluva long time.

Opening the card, Mike figured to get the rest of it over with, too. The picture on the front, a simple Happy Birthday greeting. But the inside shredded what was left of his emotional strength.

Mike-

"Happily Ever After's are still there...You just need to believe."

Love,

Tina

She was his "Happily Ever After." But his nightmares would overpower her happiness and eventually extinguish her effervescent light. That was why he'd sent her away.

CHAPTER TWO

EARLY JUNE—

Perusing the class, Mike Linder didn't see her. She was on the class roster, he'd checked the assignment sheet last night when he returned home. Why did he care? He shouldn't but he couldn't stop caring about Tina Johnston. Glancing at his watch, she had two minutes to get to class before he counted her tardy. Three late arrivals to any class in Shield training and you were kicked out or reprimanded, depending on how far along in the program you were. Part of him wished for her to be late—he'd find a way to dole out his own form of punishment for Tina.

Haven't you tortured her enough, Mike? He couldn't shake the image of the last time they'd been together, intimately. It had been two months but the memory still haunted him. She'd innocently woken him up from his usual nightmare, and he'd grabbed her, bruising her delicate wrist. Squeezing his eyes shut until he saw bursts of colors on black, he fought to erase the image of seeing the purplish-black bruise upon such pale beauty.

There'd been fear in her eyes in that single moment, but she forgave him instantly and told him she was fine. She hadn't been fine. She'd been marred by a beast! Why couldn't she see him as he was? She deserved so much more than a lifetime of pain with him. That was why he'd had to lie to her when she'd dropped by with his birthday gift.

Tina picked that moment to walk into the classroom. She stopped at the sight of him leaning against the podium. The startled "o"of her sweet pink lips stopped his heart. But he noticed she recovered soon enough. Her jaw tightened as she sauntered to an empty seat at the back of the room.

"Running late, Ms. Johnston?"

"It won't happen again, Mr. Linder." Tina bristled.

Another student walked in and sat down but Mike didn't reprimand him. There was a perverse need to egg Tina. Any sort of contact with her, even negative, was still contact.

"Good afternoon, I'm Mike Linder of Linder Electronics and Communications. I'm here to introduce you to some of the latest technology in safety securities and weapons against the Vamiers. The next three days you will learn everything you need to know about keeping your Dacian counterpart safe during a possible Vamier attack. I suggest an hour of study each night because you will be tested in a hands-on scenario sometime next week. If you have any questions you can contact me through my private email listed on the on-line blackboard for this class." His glance roamed around the room but landed on Tina.

She appeared to be typing away on her digital notepad until she raised her head. Their eyes locked. Those baby blues of hers no longer held anything for him. Had she given up on him? Mike's heart broke as he thought of her no longer caring.

Mike, she didn't break your heart. You let it be broken. You have no one to blame but yourself. He'd punch his conscience in the nose later.

* * *

His head came off with the force of her round house kick. Tina looked around worriedly at the empty room, wondering if she would have to pay for damages to the dummy mannequin.

Maybe she could super glue it back on and no one would notice.

Swallowing a drink of water, she wiped at the sweat beading her forehead. She'd been at this for hours. Yes, she had a purpose for her actions. Mike Linder. He'd treated her as if she were nothing more to him than a lowly Plebe when he'd seen her in his classroom. After all they'd shared. It hurt. The result, anger. She took it out on "Bob the Mannequin."

The door opened. Rick Delvante, owner of Livedel Enterprise entered. The man still scared the piss out of her. So serious and demanding. Nibbling her lip nervously, she watched as he walked around the decapitated practice dummy.

"I'm...I'm so sorry, Mr. Delvante. I'll replace it as soon as I can...or take it out of my paycheck."

He raised his brows at her, and the usual stern glare turned into one of fascination and awe. "You think I'm in here to reprimand you for kicking 'Bob's' head off?"

"You're not?"

"Tina," he said as his mouth curved with a smile. "I've been monitoring your activities lately. I don't know where you get your fierce strength, but you hide it well inside your petite, innocent exterior. I'm impressed. You would have made a hell of a Shield."

Gazing up at the ceiling and walls, she noticed for the first time a small dome shaped object in the far corner tiles overhead. Great! Now she felt self-conscious.

Wait. What had he said?

"I would have?" What had she done wrong? "I promise I'll

replace Bob. I didn't mean to kick his head off. Don't take me off the team."

"That's not it, Tina." He opened his mouth as if to say more on the subject but retreated. "I need to see you in my office tomorrow. I think it's time for you to understand some things that are about to happen."

"You mean in my training?" She was confused. Rick had an oddity in which he talked in riddles. But she supposed a man who was alive before the birth of Christ had every right to talk however he wanted.

"Training, yes. But not as a Shield." He nodded at her. "Carry on."

Tina wasn't sure how. All of a sudden her topsy-turvy life just took another spin. She had the leader of the immortal world telling her she was training for a new position? And not as a Shield? What else was there for a mortal person to train for at Livedel?

All she'd wanted to do was to become a Shield so she might be able to prove to Mike she could take care of him. She would be his Shield and find a way to win his heart. But that bubble burst. Screw him and his attitude. She wasn't someone to be looked down upon and treated like an infant.

She'd stopped crying weeks ago, but still felt lost. Even her best friend, Marilyn couldn't be here with her. She'd been busy helping Professor Vamier rebuild his home she'd destroyed, working on her new relationship and learning the ropes of handling an ancient government. Marilyn didn't have time to deal with a heartbroken friend.

Tina didn't blame her. How many times had Marilyn baled her out of heartbreak? Too many to count. She'd always been a sucker for wounded souls, thinking she could nurture and protect them from their own demons. In the end, they didn't want to be fixed. They only wanted a good time for awhile—until the next shiny new toy caught their eye.

She hit the punching bag sending the large canvas bag to sway on its thick linked chain. Mike Linder, he'd been different from all the others she'd dated. He was older, more mature—Tina snorted. *Yeah, that was an understatement.* She hit the bag again.

He'd been protective, keeping her safe from those who'd been out to harm her and Marilyn, the creatures she was here to learn how to fight now. Ironic. She'd stayed at his house, up in the Catoctin Mountain range for nearly three months. She'd learned to sleep during the day so she could be up with him at night, much to his dismay at first. But then after a few weeks he showed a real interest in her.

Remembering their talks about his past growing up in Texas and his days as the "all American" high school football hero, nothing like the brooding disasters she'd dated in high school and college. But in the end, Mike suffered real torture. A Vietnam War survivor. He'd witnessed death first hand. Lost his life and regained it from the creatures she'd been training to destroy—vampires.

After the way he'd treated her two months ago, there was one vampire in particular she wanted to destroy—Mike Linder.

She hit the bag with so much force it rocked back like a massive pendulum and returned in momentum to knock her on her butt. Tina looked up at the camera's dome and stuck her tongue out. Let Rick reprimand her now. She didn't give a rat's ass.

She'd had enough workout for today. Finishing her bottle of water, she tossed it in the recycling bin and headed to the showers. She had a test in Vampire Psychology in less than an hour. Having dealt with Mike for a few months, she should have no problem acing the test.

* * *

After two months, Tina still hadn't gotten used to living on sight. The Livedel compound was secluded up in the mountains of western Maryland in an old military instillation. Everyone training for the job of Shield had to give up their public domains and become a secluded entity. Lodging was provided in private apartments fit for corporate executives. This was definitely not run by government funding.

Rick Delvante went to great lengths to create a haven for both immortals and the mortals who guided them. That was where her training was coming in. To be chosen as a Shield meant the utmost respect. Very few were selected by Rick Delvante himself as a possible candidate. Why he thought she was a probable contestant, was beyond her. Okay, so she knew about the Dacians and Vamiers, two ancient immortal clans who were each other's worst enemy. And her friend Marilyn and her fiancé Draylon were an off-shoot of the immortal Dacian warrior guides known as Zmei.

It freaked Tina out thinking about the first time Marilyn shifted into her wolf form. Now, not only could her friend become a wolf, but she shifted into the form of a dragon. As Marilyn's maid of honor for the wedding in a few months, maybe she'd be able to see her friend as a Zmeu. Tina wanted pictures but due to heightened security issues, pictures of immortals and definitely of the new Zmei, were not allowed. Besides, if actual pictures somehow got out about dragons, the human race would explode in terror or worse, want a Zmei for themselves.

Walking across the campus to her apartment, she stopped at their market square. Delvante had created a structure of modern European delight in which a bricked pedestrian area surrounded by trees, gaslights and stores for both mortals and immortals, constituted the village. Tina stopped at the patisserie and picked out a loaf of French bread and chocolate croissants for breakfast before heading over to the butchers for Italian salami and speck. The cheese and wine shops were next. She dropped by the open market produce stand and picked up fruits and vegetables. Dining and shopping were a daily occurrence. She learned to eat only fresh, whole foods. Life was good here at Livedel—but it came at a cost. She'd given up her normal, civilian life.

"*Good evening, Miss Johnston—I hope you are well.*"

Each Shield apartment was wired with a personal assistant programmed into the speaker system. "Yes I am well, thank you, Doris. And you?"

She called the voice "Doris"because it sounded like a concerned mother every time it spoke. Doris was a good name. Tina forgot that it wasn't human at times.

"*I am well.*"

There was a pause as Tina put her groceries away. "Any messages for me?"

"Yes. Miss Marilyn called to tell you she has some new ideas for the wedding. She has sent them to your laptop. Would you like me to bring them up?"

"I'll look at them later. I have some homework to study first."

"No. First you will eat a healthy dinner. You haven't eaten since breakfast, you need one more glass of water to meet your daily intake and your sugar levels are low. May I suggest, based on what you have available, a filet of Tilapia coated in a tortilla chip crust, roasted asparagus drizzled with olive oil and garlic with a glass of Pinot Grigio—after your water intake is met."

The only bad thing about having an automated assistant was they could be worse than mothers. But nine-times out of ten, what they prescribed was dead on balls accurate.

"All right." Tina sighed. "Are you going to make it for me, too?"

"You know I am not able to do so. I can preheat the oven if you wish to broil—"

"I'm fine, Doris—just giving you a hard time."

"I see. Very well. Anything else I may prepare for you, Miss?"

"Set the temperature in the apartment for seventy-two degrees and could you play me some Al Jarreau?"

"Very well. Enjoy your evening, Miss Johnston."

"You too, Doris."

Doris had eyes and ears. She knew it would be senseless to deviate from her plan. So Tina drank a full glass of water and began preparing the meal set forth by Doris. She did fix a glass of wine—after her water intake and nibbled on cheese while fixing everything else. But listening to Al Jarreau's, "We're in This Love Together", had her dancing around the galley kitchen prior to the wine kicking in.

While the fish was broiling, she quickly changed into the US NAVY t-shirt Mike had given her as a loaner. It was the one thing of his she took with her. He hadn't asked for it back and she figured it was a fair trade—she took his favorite shirt—he had her heart. Let his new fling find her own damn shirt.

She poured another glass of wine and drank it down. She shouldn't care. What hurt the most was having spent so much time figuring out a birthday gift for him, taking it to his house, only to have him greet her at the door looking like he'd just been rolled. He wouldn't let her in because "he had company." She'd wanted to drop the gift right then and there, but she'd stammered something about wanting him to have it. He probably never even opened it. It might be in the trash for all she knew.

And now she had to put up with him for the next two days as he taught the class? How cruel could fate be? Did he have a clue how difficult it was for her to walk into the classroom upon seeing him there in his tight fitting khaki slacks and his sport shirt stretched over his broad chest and shoulders? His rugged blond, "all American" good looks didn't distract from his overall straight forward heart breaking bad boy persona. She'd been victim of how bad he could be—and he was very, very good at being bad.

He'd told the class that if they had any questions to contact him on his private email. Well, she had questions galore. But none of them pertained to the class work. She wanted to know why he could just hook up with someone else at the drop of a hat. He never said anything about not wanting to see her anymore...

Well, that wasn't true. He'd told her she didn't deserve him, that he was a monster with too many demons inside of him and that she would be better off on her own. She didn't agree. She wouldn't even listen to his reasoning. But even that didn't change things. No, it wasn't until he'd had the nightmare. When she'd tried to wake him up he'd grabbed her wrist and tried to attack her. She'd been frightened but knew he suffered PTSD from something that happened in Vietnam forty years ago.

She'd tried to hide the bruise from him, but once he'd seen it he knew. She even tried to cover it up. But he knew and had Marilyn and Draylon come to take her to be examined, never to be allowed back into his home or his life.

Tears pooled in her eyes. Wiping them she cursed herself. She was done crying over Mike. He'd abandoned her. She'd tried to contact him and he'd refused to answer his phone, didn't return texts, so when she went to give him his birthday gift—she knew it was really over. He'd moved on.

Damn him.

Tina managed to choke down dinner, but her heart was no longer in the mood. Doris would know and reprimand her and possibly get word to Rick that she wasn't eating. It was as bad as having Big Brother around. But there were never any real issues and the assistants were programmed for protection and safety, not spying.

She cleaned up the kitchen and sat down with the rest of the wine. If it didn't help the heartache then maybe it would help her sleep. Clicking on her digital pad, she looked over her assignments and worked on those that were due. Finally she gave in and studied the information Mike had for them to go over. She had questions—oh so many questions. But she refused to give him the satisfaction of needing him—for anything.

CHAPTER THREE

Mike took another swig from his beer. It was his third in less than an hour. It didn't matter, he couldn't get drunk, not by actual alcohol. Staring at the snow globe on the mantle he grimaced.

How many times in the past few months had he wanted to smash the glass decoration against his rock wall? The ache in his heart had him actually breaking down—disgusted at himself for what he'd done to Tina, what he'd become and what he'd lost all those years ago. He'd let himself go that night in a violent rage. He attacked a drunk in downtown Frederick and fed off of him, getting inebriated the only way his kind could and nearly draining the man in the process.

Maybe it would've been better if he had. Then he'd be out of his misery, just another rogue Vamier needing to be killed. Delvante would have sent someone to hunt him down and kill him.

He stood. Tossing the empty bottle across the room into his recycling bin, he walked over to the fireplace mantle and gazed upon the beautiful gift. The details of the chapel at the United States Naval Academy stood center around a wintery scene with trees and the open area he knew intimately. Gently picking it up from the shelf he shook it, setting the glittering flakes of iridescent fake snow into a blizzard swirling around the tiny replica.

He should've never told Tina about his dreams and how he wanted to find a woman and one day marry her at the chapel. Why had he? He'd never shared himself with any other woman so intimately as he had with Tina. Most of the women he'd known didn't know what he was. Tina knew all of it and hadn't walked away.

"No, instead you attacked her and then sent her away like a coward," he spat viciously as his hand clenched tightly around the base of the globe, shaking.

Diligent control and the deep breathing techniques his friend Draylon taught him over the years calmed him enough to put the globe back on the shelf in one piece. He'd kept it, not as an intimate reminder of what he'd had but as punishment for the hell he'd caused the one woman who'd made him feel like a real man after decades of self-torment and isolation.

Going to his laptop again, he checked the on-line blackboard from his class. Only a few questions but nothing from the one person he wanted to hear from. He answered the questions and once he was finished, thought about going for a night ride.

Above, the doorbell to the house rang. He'd created a façade to cover his actual living quarters built into the mountainside overlooking the Catoctin valley. Like Batman in his Bat Cave, his "house"hid a multitude of secrets.

Few knew where he lived, Draylon and now his fiancée, Marilyn, Rick Delvante, and Tina Johnston. Part of him hoped it was the latter but prayed it wasn't. There was no way he'd be able to resist her if she stood at his door with her big blue eyes. She was the only ray of sunlight he'd found.

Anxiously Mike glanced at the video screen showing the surrounding view of his home. He was Rick Delvante's surveillance expert for a reason. He knew what it took to create a secure environment for the Dacian and his people. The ancient

Dacian leader stood at his front door.

Not really who he was expecting...or needing right now, and the leather case dangling at his side did not indicate he was here for a game of billiards or darts. Rick was here on business.

The doorbell rang again. He could pretend he wasn't home, but if Rick found out he'd been ignored, he could expectunpleasant results in the end. Sighing, Mike pushed the button to unlatch the security lock on his front door, letting in the one man most people fought to keep out.

Going over to the bar, he poured a glass of Semi-globin, Dr. Jon Johnston's creation of artificial hemoglobin that most Dacian fostered Vamiers learned to indulge in when the real stuff wasn't available. Though Rick wasn't a Vamier, he did enjoy a glass or two when visiting his Vamier friends.

"You look like hell, Mike," Rick stated as he walked into the large "man cave"Mike had made for himself.

"Nice to see you too, Rick." Mike handed the other man a glass and poured himself one.

"Some of Doc's special vintage?"

"I only bring it out when you show up." Nodding to the satchel in Rick's hand, Mike leaned casually against the bar. "I take it you are not here to shoot the shit." He took a sip of the bloody concoction. It wasn't the same as the actual real stuff but safer and just as nourishing. Delvante Vamiers were given permission to feed off mortals twice a month and were usually provided with a subject brought to them at a designated place. No harm to the victim and their memories of the event were immediately deleted.

"No." Rick walked over to the Italian leather sectional and sat, taking great care in removing a file from his attaché case. "I need you to look at something." He held out a thick binder to him.

Mike approached cautiously. The concerned look on the old man's face had him wary. All he could think of was that he'd pissed him off somehow and this was the "calm" before all hell broke loose.

"What's this?"

"Sit down...I think you'll find this rather interesting."

Sitting, he took the file from Rick, never taking his eyes off of the powerful man. He trusted him but never got used to the mysterious ways he worked.

The file weighed heavy in his hand but holding it caused him to shutter as unknown fear took hold of him. Setting his glass to the side table he opened it. A name, a face...different but the same as he remembered, but in different surroundings.

"No. This...can't be...is this who I think it is?" Mike stuttered after a few moments of shock.

Rick shrugged. "You tell me."

Jack Tabor, CEO of Tabor Financials.

Ice cold water ran through his veins. Did he look as pale as he felt? Shock, remorse, anger...decades of emotions sucker punched him in his most vulnerable place. The file held his past, his nightmare, his sanity, and it stared back at him mockingly.

"What do you know about *this* man?" Mike asked warily.

"Only what's in the file. Mostly about his company, profits and financial profile." Rick studied his nails. "But he seems to have more than a financial business. Rumor has it he's accumulated a rash of rogue Vamiers and has started his own clan. We can't have various clans without being sanctioned under the Council of the Guardians. I'm keeping a close eye on his last reported sightings and..."

Mike waited for Rick to continue, but he didn't, just stared at him with something akin to sympathy. Mike hated that. "And what? This isn't him, this isn't Johnny."

Silence strung around them like a spider's web with the spider waiting to catch its dinner. Mike knew Rick didn't believe him. The man could read minds if he needed to. He didn't believe himself. The man in the folder looked like his friend, Johnny Tabor, but it couldn't be him, maybe a son or grandson he didn't know about?

"Well, whatever the case, we need to keep an eye on him." Rick handed him another envelope. This time a military/government shotgun folder. Mike unwrapped the red string, holding the flap closed. Pulling out the enclosed dossier pictures, they scattered across his coffee table. The man had his back to the camera in most shots, a side profile in a few...Johnny...

No, Johnny Tabor was dead. He'd been killed in action in Vietnam. They were all dead...they were all dead...

"Mike? Are you all right?" Rick's voice sounded so far away. The echo of it ricocheting off of the stone walls but falling on deaf ears. Instead he heard the distant bombs and shelling of shadows past.

"They've been gone a long time, sir. Do you think we should move in?" Chief Sharp whispered from his flank.

Mike checked his watch. It had been longer than anticipated. Dark night had taken over the dusky twilight they'd had when Johnny jumped at the chance to take his team in. He knew he shouldn't have let him go in there. They had no clue what they were up against. A Gook camp holding American troops, that was all they knew. There hadn't been any sounds of major gun fire or action of any kind—from their vantage point. They should have heard something. Even their line of communication was dead.

He motioned for his SEAL team to follow, giving them hand signals as to their tasks. The eerie quiet of the jungle heightened all of their senses. That is what they trained for, Special Operations, go in, get them and bring them home.

His heart pounded in his ears. He could hear the blood flowing, the adrenalin surging. This wasn't a drill or team game—this was for real.

The clearing came upon them within the half hour. They weren't sure what to expect upon arrival, but the abandoned site was not on their plans at all. Splitting his team up, he gave silent orders to search the compound before heading in the direction of the main outpost.

Night made it nearly impossible to see anything. The moon held just enough illumination to cast shadows and stir the palm ferns of the undergrowth around them. Charleys hid in the undergrowth, waiting. Mike stirred at the slightest breeze or ruffle. His eyes wide, taking in what light he could.

Making his way to the main building of bamboo and a thatched roof, he took his time approaching the entrance. Upon entering, the ghastly sight had him nearly upchucking his latest MRE. A man lay slumped over the short wave radio at what appeared to be a communications office. With the barrel of his rifle, Mike nudged the body and it fell to the floor in a deathly heap—blood everywhere—from a ripped out throat. The eyes of the Viet Cong were gruesomely open in shock at whatever was the last thing he saw.

"Sir."

Mike jumped out of his skin at the sound of one of his men peering around the open door. "They're dead. They're all dead."

"Mike!" He felt the sharp sting to his face, and it took a moment to register. But when it did he went into action.

His assailant was in a chokehold waiting for his nose to be shattered into his skull.

Rick stared back at him. There was no fear. There wasn't anything reflected in his eyes. His posture relaxed, his face firm. Mike eased his arm from around his neck and took a step back. Mike awaited his fate. Rick Delvante killed men for less.

Rick adjusted his suit and brushed himself off as if he'd fallen down.

"Go over this folder as soon as you can. I want you to find out what you can on him," Rick said as he focused on picking off a piece of imaginary lint from his Armani sleeve.

Mike didn't talk. He couldn't. He nodded and stood silently

as Rick let himself out the way he'd come in, leaving him to live another damned day.

* * *

"What?" Tina sat forward in the chair as she contemplated the news she'd just received from Rick Delvante. "I'm a what?"

"You are what the Dacian clans call theImmortal's Angel."

"Is that some high ranking Shield?"

Rick pinched the bridge of his nose and closed his eyes. "Stop with the Shield business. No. This has nothing to do with being a Shield or Shield Training, Tina."

Worrying the inside of her cheek, she wondered if it was possible to chew through her own face. "So I'm an Angel as in wings, halos and harps?"

Rick sighed. "Michelangelo was so wrong in his interpretations." He perched on the sofa across from Tina, tempeling his fingers beneath his chin. "No. Not exactly."

"I can't fly, don't have Heavenly connections..."

"No...and yes." Rick became excited when she guessed certain parts.

"Just tell me, Mr. Delvante. This beating around the bush is driving me insane." Tina shook her head wearily.

"I'll try. There is so much you don't understand about our kind, our history and heritage. It's difficult for most mortals to comprehend." He let out a breath. "What do you know of our kind? What has my daughter, Marilyn told you?"

"Let's see. The Dacians were great warriors. Other lands and tribes feared your mysterious ways and your dragons, known as Zmei, who fought beside you in battle. The gods gifted the Zmei to your people in exchange for a maiden every five harvest seasons to become a Zmei mate."

"So far, so good..."

"Your brother Aiden angered the gods by sending in his own Army of men to steal away the recent Zmei bride he'd fallen in love with. She was actually one of the Dacian goddesses in disguise, pregnant with the last blood of the Zmei clan. The Zmei were destroyed by Aiden's troops—all except one, Draylon, Marilyn's fiancé."

"Good, good..."

"The gods were pissed off and divided the clan—one half that of the wolf, half of the clan crest and the other half, vampire—demons who live off the blood of their fellow man and are shunned by the Sun god for eternity."

"I am pleased. You are well versed in our history." Rick nodded approvingly.

"So where do I fit in? Something tells me there is a new chapter about to unfold."

"History unfolds all the time. Today's news is tomorrows past. But when you are immortal, time stands still. We don't age but the world turns around us. Cultures change, politics and religion converge, technology and science blend with nature and fantasy."

Was he talking in riddles again? Tina tried to follow him. Some of what he said made sense in a weird sort of way. "Can we get to the part where I am theImmortal's Angel?"

He nodded. “Of course.” Rick stood up and went to his large desk. “Our gods were angered by what had happened, but as the years progressed and we found our own ways, divided as they were, Zamoxelis the Great came out of hiding and foretold of an angel he would send when all the gods found fault with the human race.”

“All the gods?”

“Yes. Since the beginning of time on Earth and when the gods created man, we were put on the Earth as protectors. We were to nurture and live in harmony with everything the gods created. And in return, we were given paradise.”

“You’re talking about Eden.”

Rick shrugged. “For us, we’ve known it as Dacia.”

“And we all fell from their grace?”

Toying with a pen on his desk blotter, he nodded.

“Are they mad now?”

“There is war in the Middle East, death and combat related to religion and politics, global warming and pollution, extinction of our most sacred brethren, the animals we were to protect and cherish. Those who are trying to bring back the world set for us by the gods are being considered to stay. Those who reach out to others are also considered.”

“What about the rest?”

“The gods will decide their eternal fate.”

“Earthquakes, famine, floods...”

“Not exactly, those are just happenstances brought on by

man himself."

"So what is my part?"

"You are the chosen one, by Zamoxelis, to help alleviate the chaos in the Vamier clan. So many have gone rogue, not being properly turned and suffering because of it. It is your duty, set forth by our god, to help them decide to move on or convert."

"Move on…as in death?"

"Yes. Technically you are considered the angel of mercy and death…a merciful death."

Tina fought to contemplate all Rick was telling her. She didn't deny the fact of there being something called theImmortal's Angel. Delvante, the Dacians, her friend being an immortal legend. Mike, sure…but her? She was mortal, she was conceived by mortal parents. It didn't make sense.

"Are you sure, I'm the one?" She didn't feel like an angel. Angels weren't confused women unsure about their life or goals. They didn't have heartaches and make choices based on their need to help and nurture…well, okay maybe that might be a small part. But there were others in the world who felt that way.

But she was going to be dealing with vampires, rogue vampires who were badass killers. They were worse than druggies hyped up on PCP. They had no conscience, only the desire to feed off of unsuspecting victims…either killing them or partially turning them, unintentionally.

Damn! That's what she had to deal with. She'd be in charge of the ones who'd been partially turned. Her job could take years. They needed to get rid of the rogue vampires first.

"I'll be encountering rogue Vamiers, too? Won't I?"

"Yes, there is that possibility. But I won't have you doing your job alone. You'll be part of a team of soldiers I send in to annihilate the rogues."

"Soldiers like...Draylon and Mike..."

"Yes. I have many teams who work for me...not just them. But you will go where I send you. For the next month or so, you will be personally trained by my staff to learn all you need to know as theImmortal's Angel. There will be physical training, mental and psychological training and interviewing our recently turned Vamiers. I want you to be able to handle most scenarios you encounter in your duties. "

"What if I encounter something I don't understand or I'm in danger that my training won't see to? What do I do then?"

Walking around the side of his desk Rick stood mere inches from her. His presence was dominant and scared her to hell. She had to remind herself this was Marilyn's father. He wouldn't hurt her. Would he?

His eyes swirled with liquid silver, his smile twisted into a semi-smile. The touch of his palm against her cheek had her inhale sharply. Like a shock to his system, his touch held a strong voltage of power.

Whoa! What was that?

"If you encounter anything outside your comfort zone, there is only one thing you can do, Christina Johnston—Pray to God."

* * *

He waited as long as he could. Mike looked out over the sea of new Shield recruits and Tina wasn't one of them. Was she avoiding him on purpose? Rick wouldn't like that. Recruits were not allowed to skip classes unless they were sick or dead. He didn't wish either on Tina.

Going to the door, he glanced up and down the empty hallway briefly to see if she might be running late. Nothing. He closed the door.

"Anyone see or hear from Christina Johnston today?" he asked the class as he shuffled his notes.

"She wasn't in my Security Class this morning," one girl piped up, popping the bubble gum she was chewing.

"She missed the morning briefing, too," a guy stated.

"Someone mentioned she might be suffering from morning sickness," another guy joked. "You know how those innocent looking ones are..."

This got a round of laughter from some of the other guys and girls, but Mike wasn't amused. Walking over to the "class clown," he picked him up by the front of his shirt and glared him down.

An eerie quiet settled over the class.

The kid's eyes bulged in fright.

"If I hear another derogatory, sexist remark about Ms. Johnston...or anyone...I will personally take you out and make sure you're never able to step foot in the Livedel Compound again."

"It...it...was a...joke, sir."

Mike lowered the kid none too gently back into his chair. “A joke?” He leaned casually against a fellow student’s desk and folded his arms. “I love a good joke. I suppose you are the class entertainer?” Mike didn’t wait for a reply. As he walked back up to the front of the class, no one talked. He didn’t even hear the sounds of breathing. “I didn’t think the joke was funny at all. I don’t tolerate sexual harassment in my class.”

He sat there, waiting for the class to breathe, move, do something. But no one moved, not even to pop their gum.

“Take out your tablets...there is a pop quiz in the documents menu.” He looked at his watch. “You have twenty minutes—and yes, I am grading it.”

“But we haven’t studied these issues,” Jokester complained as he looked to his tablet.

“Ten minutes...” Mike amended.

The grumbling and shuffling from the rest of the class were punctuated with vicious glares at the comedian. But the breathing had begun again as they all rapidly focused on the multiple-guess quiz he’d set up.

Sitting on the corner of his desk, Mike’s mind began to wander. The joke hadn’t been funny—but was it true? It had been a few months since they’d been together...Hell, who was he kidding? He couldn’t breed. He’d been infertile since being changed. Vamiers weren’t capable of impregnating anyone, not even someone from their own species. But if Tina was pregnant...it wasn’t his. Mike’s jaw tingled with the itch to take blood, anyone’s.

* * *

Out of the thirty-five pupils in his class, so far there were only three students who passed the test. Mr. Comedian was still sitting, puzzling over the questions.

The few students who'd passed had their documents sent back to him within the first five minutes—and were correct. He looked out over his class and made subtle eye contact with those who knew they'd passed. Nodding at them he motioned to the door...they were free to go. Others looked up from their tablets in confusion as the small group gathered their things and left

"Five more minutes."

Mike could smell the sweat from the rest as they tried to answer the questions faster. He didn't flinch though. He didn't want them to know anything...yet.

At the seven minute mark, Mr. Comedian's test was sent. Mike looked at the document. He'd answered all the questions, randomly...the answers were legitimate and correct which was unfortunate for him. The student smiled cockily and rose to leave.

Mike stopped him before he managed to get past his desk and motioned for him to sit back down. The guy gestured wildly and slumped in his seat.

"One minute," he announced to the class as he glanced at his watch.

A minute later his watch alarm went off. "Tablets down."

A cacophony of tablets being placed on the desks mingled with mutters and groans of unfinished questions and curses of how stupid the questions were.

"Those of you still seated...this is a strike against your ratings in Shield Training. If this is your third strike, please go to the admissions office and let them know you will be leaving the compound permanently."

"This is bullshit!" Mr. Comedian stood up and exclaimed. "I answered those questions, and I know for a fact they are correct."

"How do you know?" He didn't wait. "If you will all look back at the top of your document...it says, what?" Mike motioned to the gum popping girl in the front of the room.

"'Type in your name and today's date and turn the test in to Mr. Linder,'" she read casually. And then it hit her and her face fell.

If they'd read the directions on the test, they all would have been done within mere seconds. The rest were bullshit questions he'd put in to see how many of the students paid attention to details. In this business, details were important.

"I call bullshit! This wasn't a fair test," his funny friend erupted.

"There is no 'fair test' in life or as a Shield. Attention to detail...everything around you, people you come into contact with, anything and everything can be detrimental to you between life and death. This is about the fairest test there is...and you're lucky enough to get out of it with your life intact," Mike instructed. "That is all."

He dismissed the rest of the students. Some, like the kid he'd dealt with, stormed out cussing and cursing him and Shield Training. He was probably on his last strike against him. Good riddance! The clan didn't need someone with his attitude anyway.

"Sir?"

A young woman who appeared intelligent but terrified of her own shadow stopped at his desk. She was the last student. Pushing her black framed glasses up on her nose she fumbled with her book bag.

"Yes. Can I help you?"

"Actually...um...I heard from a friend of mine, who knows a girl, who has a class with Tina Johnston that she was assigned a special task from Mr. Delvante early this morning. But I could be mistaken..."

Mike studied the girl. He wouldn't put it past Rick to do something like that, but in the middle of Shield Training? None of them were ready to take on any mission so soon. Why would he jeopardize Tina like that?

"Thank you...um..."

"Gail, sir. Gail Weston."

"Well Ms. Weston, thank you for the information. I'll look into it. I would hate for Ms. Johnston to have a strike against her for no reason." He stopped. "This isn't your last strike, is it?"

"No sir. This is my first."

"I'm sorry that you had to receive one." He truly was. She might take it much too hard as a failure. He'd known some of his shipmates in the Naval Academy who couldn't deal with failure of any kind.

"It's okay, sir. It was a valuable lesson to learn. I'll be more aware of things now. Hopefully I can use it to better myself." She gave a slight smile.

Gail Weston was interesting. He liked her attitude about learning. She had what his mother always referred to as "quiet beauty." She wasn't a model, but if given the chance she would be very pretty. Her smile was enough to show that.

"Well, I wish you the best in the remainder of your training. I hope to see you out in the field someday soon."

"Thank you, sir."

There was a spring in her step and did he imagine it or had her head tilted up a bit more? Mike wasn't sure, but something told him she would become an excellent Shield.

* * *

"You sent her out already? What kind of asinine call was that? You know damn well she's not capable of fending for herself out there in our world."

Rick stood behind his desk. He was barely six foot to Mike's towering six foot-four and yet the man could kill him in less time than it took to utter the words...if he wanted to.

"It amazes me Mike that after forty years, you still have a death wish." Rick eyed him. "I'd have put you out of your misery a long time ago for your insolence, but I know that is what you've wished for. I refuse to give you the peace you think you'll find in death."

Mike crossed his arms in defiance. "I don't give a damn about me, I'm talking about Christina Johnston, she's too innocent and naïve where our world is concerned."

"I'll make the decisions in this corporation. If I didn't think she could handle herself I wouldn't have put her in the position."

"Damn it, Rick!" Mike slammed his fist down on the hard, mahogany desk that separated the two of them. "She is not a Shield."

"Did I say I sent her out as a Shield...no, you assumed." Walking around his desk, the clan leader sat on the edge and toyed with his pen holder. "I have her training in another field. She's not meant to be a Shield."

Mike narrowed his eyes on Rick. He'd trusted the man most of his immortal life but now, hell with things happening with the ancient Dacian clans and the news of his relationship with his CFO over a quarter of a century ago...many of the clan members were beginning to doubt some of the decisions Rick Delvante made.

"You sent her back to the mortal lifestyle?"

"Where I sent her is no concern of yours, Mike."

Rick's indifference to the subject had Mike's jaw aching. He fought his fangs from elongating and frustratingly taking a bite out of the man, just to spit him out.

"Where in the hell is she, Rick? No more games."

"She's safe, which is more than I can say for you right now. You're about to end up a blond crispy critter if you don't cool your blood down."

"And as I said...I don't give a fuck about me. Tina is who I am concerned about."

"Really?" Rick studied his professionally manicured fingers. "I thought you stopped caring when you told her to get the hell out of your life."

"Fuck you, Rick."

Very few people knew about the short relationship he'd had with Tina. He didn't want her effected by the clan or anyone in it. He'd been assigned to protect her when Marilyn Reddlin had been in danger. The two women had been roommates and best friends. Marilyn had let herself be captured by the Vamiers and Draylon had put him in charge of keeping Tina safe while he'd gone after her. Mike had no intentions of anything more than being her protector, but she'd gotten under his skin and given him a glimpse of sunshine in his darkened world. She'd been more potent than any drug Draylon could have prescribed—a drug he had no right getting addicted to.

Now Rick was taunting him, damning him for doing what he'd known was the right thing to do. He'd sent her away so she would be safe from creatures like him. Only to have Rick send her God knew where.

The slow nod from his superior told him this wasn't over.

"You're leaving for Landstuhl, Germany tonight. I think you need to get out of my sight for a while before we end up enemies." Rick pulled out a packet from his desk file. "There's been rumors of wounded soldiers having been turned and left to fend for themselves on the Middle East battlefields. They've been spotted arriving at the European Medical facility in Germany. For the past few months, Trenchfoot has been taking care of hunting some of them down after being turned or semi-turned. But we've lost contact with him. It's not like him to not stay in touch. I need you to go find him. You know his private life better than most of my teams. If things are going bad, he'll talk to you. He trusts you. You can help him with the wounded soldiers who've been turned."

"You want me to work with wounded soldiers? Are you out of your fucking mind?"

Mike knew what Rick was up to. Send the broken man into his own hell to help others cope. Yeah well, he was the worst one to put in that position.

"You will go...or I'll make sure Tina's training is more complex. The choice is yours."

This time Mike didn't hold back. With his teeth bared, he hurled his two hundred thirty pound frame at Rick Delvante to do some real harm. The elder suddenly turned into a black furred beast of a wolf and went for Mike's jugular. The two tumbled off the desk and fought, beast to beast, until ice cold water poured over them like a tidal wave.

Rebecca DeRynold stood before them. A short, curly haired pixie who looked like an Amazon warrior princess. Her chest puffed out, and her eyes glared at the two of them lying on the ground, bloody gashes oozing all over the floor from their various wounds.

"If you two expect me to clean up this mess, think again. Now get your shit together Mike and take off before Rick gets his second wind."

Rebecca didn't take crap from anyone. That was why Rick

liked her and had hired her a few years back as his personal assistant. She was petite but mighty and had a master black belt in Karate from the school of Kicking Your Ass. She bent down to tend to Rick who lay naked, bleeding from his arm and chest where Mike hadgotten a good bite into Rick's shoulder and pecs.

Mike wiped the blood from his lips, not even caring about the gash in his own side, it would heal within moments. Picking up the large manila envelope Rick had given him moments ago he turned to leave, cursing the fact he would do whatever it took to keep Rick from sending Tina into harm's way.

CHAPTER FOUR

The five mile runs had become easier over the first few weeks of training but when Rebecca DeRynolds bumped it up to ten because the five miles *had* become easier, Tina knew she would die or kill Becca.

"Come on you, Wuss! My grandmother can run further than you...and she's dead," Becca called out five paces ahead of her while turning around and jogging backwards.

All Tina wanted to do was puke blood. Her lungs felt like shards of glass were ripping them to shreds and this was the beginning of the day.

Rick hadn't been joking when he said Rebecca was the best physical trainer. Why this girl hadn't become a Drill Instructor in the Marine Corp—for the guys, she wasn't sure.

No longer were her days scheduled a neat and tidy eight to three Shield Training. No, Becca had her up—day one of her training at four o'clock in the morning. Hell, the Vamiers hadn't even gone to bed yet.

Starting out with a five mile jog right off the bat. Tina hadn't run in years—not since high school track. She believed she should only run if chased, and then it depended on who was chasing her. In her line of work, rogue vampires.

The run was followed by an obstacle course made for super human guerilla warfare through the forests of the Catoctin Mountains. Becca liked to slip little surprises in along the way, like a Vamier she'd asked to add to the challenge or possibly one of the Dacian wolf shifters. Each day was different, a different trail, a different scenario, or nothing at all. Tina didn't know what to expect.

This was followed by a half an hour breakfast, whichconsisted of a protein shake and two glasses of water, before hitting a five minute shower.

But that wasn't all of her day. No, her day was only beginning at that point. Academic classes, and unlike the thirty to thirty-five students all training to be Shields, she was alone.

Dacian philosophy, mythology, ancient deities and rituals—she wondered if she could get extra college course credits for these. The one on one was a blessing, otherwise she'd be in the back of the room falling asleep as she tried to look interested.

The three classes were followed by a pure protein lunch, no carbs at all and more water. Becca picked up her training again after eating, for a refresher course in Karate and taught her Brazilian Jujitsu. Knives, swords and weaponry were added, all under Becca's tutelage. By the end of June, Tina wasn't sure if she should try out as the next Jedi Master or a Matrix agent.

Her refrigerator was nearly bare, compared to what it had been. She reached for a bottle of water and downed it in two gulps.

"Hello Miss Tina. How was your training today?"

"Hello Doris, Hell as usual," she replied, wiping sweat from her forehead and face with her tank top. "Can't talk now. I have just enough time to take a shower before heading for meditation and Dacian craft."

"I suggest a salad or at least a peanut butter sandwich be-

fore heading out. Your weight is dropping rapidly. You have lost another three pounds, bringing your total weight loss to twenty-five pounds since your recent training started."

"But I am maintaining muscle mass, right?"

"Yes. Though you are down another dress size. I suggest a shopping trip might be in order soon."

Well there were perks to the physical training she'd been going through. She fist pumped the air excitedly.

She literally had only moments to shower and change before heading back out the door. Grabbing an all-natural granola bar and another bottle of water she said good-bye to Doris and headed out for more training.

* * *

"Tonight we are working on your actual turning skills," her Angel instructor/sensei indicated as the short haired woman in a flowing white caftan led her down the hospital corridor. "We have a few recently turned patients who are in limbo. Usually our patients aren't given a choice, but with you, they now have a true say in their destiny."

Most of her mental training and psychological classes led her to this moment. Her true calling as theImmortal's Angel. She would guide their souls on to eternal life, one way or another.

The patient rooms were basically set up like an Intensive Care Unit. The patients, being held in a state of comatose until a decision could be formed based on medical criteria as to how and when they could be turned.

A young police officer had been shot and left for dead on the side of the highway until a rogue vampire had come by to turn him. It wasn't just military that were victims.

"He's been here only a few days. A prime candidate," her sensei told her. "What you need to do is lay your hands on the two vital organs of life. His head and his heart. Only by doing so can you make a clear connection into the world in which they are trapped right now."

"What happens once I do?"

Her instructor smiled and shrugged. "I cannot say. I am not theImmortal's Angel. That is for you to find out once the connection is made."

Thanks? Tina's confidence sank to her toes. She'd been told there'd never been an Immortal's Angel before her...ever. But still, she'd hoped for some sort of knowledge to base her next steps on.

The man's pale, cold features disturbed her, but she followed through, placing her left hand on his forehead and her right over his slightly beating heart.

"Cleanse your mind of all your inner thoughts. Breathe through the transition. Inhale as you transport into his mind and hold onto his heart." Her sensei's words floated over her like a trance, echoing quietly as she found herself in a dark portal.

An illuminating light appeared around her, lighting the way. The uniformed man sat on an outcropping of darkness, his head bowed, his hands between his knees. He looked up, shielding his eyes from the sudden brightness.

"Hello," Tina ventured kindly.

"Hello," he echoed. "Where am I?"

"I'm assuming somewhere between life and death."

"Why?"

"What was the last thing you remember?"

He thought momentarily. "I was approaching a vehicle I'd pulled over along 81 south out of Maryland. I asked the man to put his hands where I could see him...I'm dead, he shot me! That bastard shot me!"

"Relax. Technically you aren't dead. There is a bit more to understand." Tina took a deep breath and continued to inform him he had been partially turned after being bitten. His laugh told her he thought she was a loon. But when she told him to touch his neck, his reaction sobered.

"You have two choices. I'm here to help guide you to either one. There are people to help you adapt to your choice if you choose to become immortal. I'm not sure on the other choice. I don't think anyone is."

"Immortal as in 'living forever'?" He contemplated that. "What's the catch?"

"You would have to give up everything you know, the people you love, your career—"

"What? Is this some sort of witness protection?"

"One might think that...only multiply that by ten." Tina nodded, considering the example.

"All of that for immortality?"

"Oh, and you'll have to drink blood and forgo daylight."

"Forever?"

"Forever," she stated.

He rubbed his jaw and thought carefully. "And you don't know what I'll find on the other side?"

Tina shrugged. "Sorry."

He sighed. "Well, I was always a night person anyway. What about sex?"

Taken aback, Tina wasn't sure what he meant. "Excuse me?"

"Will I still be able to have sex?"

"Um..." She thought of Mike. Yeah, that wasn't a problem. "Yes? But you will never be able to produce offspring."

"Sounds good to me...where do I sign up?" He stood, clapping his hands together.

"Whoa! Really. You don't want to think about your other option?"

"You said you didn't know what it offered. I kind of figure if I actually die I'll still be in limbo."

"Why's that?"

"Well, darlin'...I'm the kind of guy that Heaven will never accept and Satan is afraid I might just kick his ass out and take over. Neither one will want me in their domain."

Allll righty then. She knew some immortals that fit that description.

"Sounds like you might just fit in with my immortal friends."

She took him by the hand and led him back the way she'd come. When she came to, exhausted and shaky from her experience, he was waking up. A medical staff were on standby to help him through the transition. Her sensei held her to give her emotional and physical support.

The slow process of coming back to reality gradually returned, and she watched the staff work fervently over their newest immortal candidate.

One person in general caught her attention. The voice and motions were so familiar...she knew them by heart.

Stepping away from her sensei, her mind tried to register the shock.

"Mom?"

Her mother looked up momentarily from her task, a reassuring smile on her face and a nod at her sensei before returning to her patient. Tina tried to hold back as her sensei escorted her from the room.

Her mother worked for Rick Delvante?

CHAPTER FIVE

MID-JULY—

The flight into Dallas/Ft. Worth was nothing like Tina expected. The Lear Jet landed smoothly, but her stomach still hadn't settled. Nerves, that's all it was. She wasn't prepared. Rick had given her less than twenty-four hours to pack and plan. A simple voicemail telling her folks she would be gone for a few months. Not that her folks would worry, since they had a direct connection to Rick Delvante.

After seeing her mother that night in the hospital room, she'd marched into Rick's office as soon as her sensei let her go. Hunger, exhaustion and emotional rage be damned. Rebecca wasn't there to block her, and by the time Rick's security staff got to her, he'd let her be and called off his dogs, or wolves as the case had been.

Frustration from a lifetime of deception and lies ate at her. To learn suddenly of who she was and why she was associated with Delvante and Livedel...had it all been a joke? A joke on her? She thought she'd lived in a normal world with normal parents and friends. Now nothing seemed to make sense and reality was becoming more of a fantasy world. Mike had been right, she was naïve when it came to the immortal world. Now that she didn't have a choice and was part of it, she had demanded answers—demanded them from the man in charge.

Rick had calmly sat down and explained to her how her parents had both worked for him for many decades, since World War II. They weren't immortal but didn't age as fast, as long as they were in a suitable environment. The Catoctin Mountain compound of Livedel was one of those rare places on Earth that time had a way of stopping completely. Dacia, the alternate timed Eden in Romania was another, as was Draylon's fortress, Eskardel in Austria. It was why he'd set up base nestled in the mountain range.

Did knowing she was living in an alternate universe make it any easier to digest? No. Did finding out her parents were actually old enough to be her great-grandparents make her feel better? No. Did knowing she was a part of it whether she wanted to be or not, a comfort? Not really. But knowing the truth and accepting it were two different things now.

She'd left that night, dragging her way back to her apartment in a fog of uncertainty. She contacted Marilyn and cried, talked, cried some more and by the end of their two hour talk, didn't feel quite so alone, knowing what her best friend had gone through herself. The physical change had been easy, the years of deception...would take awhile. Marilyn thanked the gods that she had Draylon to help her understand. Did that make Tina feel any better personally, nope.

Tina sighed and realized she now had a mission in life beyond bookkeeping. She'd been put on the Earth to help those who couldn't help themselves. She looked to that as a redeeming factor in her topsy-turvy fantasy life.

The hatch opened and the flight attendant dropped the stairs. Gathering her purse and wits close to her, Tina tried for professional decorum. She wasn't sure what to expect once she stepped off the plane. Turning to look behind her, she had the weirdest feeling that nothing would be the same, ever again.

She'd been sent undercover as a bookkeeper, not to do Jack Tabor's books but to find out anything about him and his movements. Rick had a suspicion that Jack Tabor wasn't just a financial wiz. He thought he might be a domesticated rogue Vamier.

Standing in the doorway, darkness and warm, humid air hit her. The lights of the private airfield winked on the black horizon. This wasn't the big international airport. A stretch limo waited for her, black and ominous, the polished chrome the only brightness to the night.

"Mr. Tabor is waiting for you, Miss."

With a weak uncertain smile, Tina nodded and said goodbye to her personal flight attendant and took her first step towards her new world with Mr. Tabor.

You wanted this. This is your adventure.

Goosebumps dotted her skin and chills pinballed around in her body. Could it be so warm and humid that she suffered from cold? It didn't make sense at all. A skycap shuttled her one suitcase to the trunk of the car and saluted the driver who stood patiently by the open limo door, waiting for her.

Closing her eyes and taking a deep breath, she took the leap of faith and crawled into the darkness looming just inside the car.

* * *

The man didn't say a word. No introduction or welcoming speech. His dark brooding appearance didn't quite match the youthful, elegant physique, the black curls. Granted, Jack Tabor might be in his mid to late twenties, but his demeanor represented a past filled with resentment and hard knocks. What terrible things did he have happen to him? Did his daddy not get him a Ferrari for his sixteenth birthday? There was no way this man wasn't born into money. He just knew how to use it to his advantage...according to his financials.

"Don't get comfortable. You aren't staying long."

"I beg your pardon?" Tina wasn't quite sure what he meant. She'd been mesmerized with the low, cosmopolitan dialect. Was she expecting a Texas drawl?

"You aren't staying long...here."

"I don't understand?"

Moments ticked by, his gaze narrowed in on her, boring into her soul.

"I have business elsewhere and you will be going with me."

"Rick Delvante said I was to take care of your business. I assumed that meant in your office."

"Never assume. And I have many offices...some are even made of steel and concrete."

Did this guy always talk in riddles? Did all immortals share that odd sense of speech? She expected someone straight forward, no nonsense. Instead, awkward silence surrounded them. He sat in the corner of the opposite side of the seat staring at her, no dissecting her.

"What are you?" he asked.

"What?"

"What are you? You're not mortal...or at least only partial."

Was this guy on acid? Totally bizarre.

"Why did Rick Delvante really send you here? You're one of his spies...or Shields, aren't you?"

"No. I am a bookkeeper. I was a bookkeeper for the Greater Baltimore Blood Bank for two years while I was finishing college..."

"...at Towson University. Yes, I know." He inhaled sharply. "Name, rank and serial number..."

"Look Mr. Tabor, I really don't know what you are talking about or exactly what you are trying to get at, but I've been assigned to be your assistant and take care of your firms accounts... according to Rick Delvante."

"I never hired you, and Rick informed me I would be sent an assistant to help me with my business—but you won't do."

She wouldn't do? Tina might not be many things, but she considered herself a gem in the office and financial environment. She'd graduated top of her class in Business Management and accounting...what right did he have to think she wasn't capable of handling the job?

"I'm not looking for an Administrative Assistant...Rick was supposed to send me an assassin."

* * *

An assassin? Did he mean a Shield? She wasn't a killer, or a hit man—or even a Shield. This was all wrong. Didn't Rick know what Jack Tabor needed?

Rubbing her forehead, Tina laughed nervously."I think there has been a terrible mix up—Mr. Delvante assumed you needed a bookkeeper. He sent me. I haven't had any training in assassinations. I do have a Black Belt in Karate, but that was back in high school...I haven't really practiced in years..."

"Rick didn't make a mistake." Jack Tabor stared at her with pinpoint accuracy. "Rick Delvante doesn't make mistakes. I'm not sure why he would send you for the job at hand, but he must have his reasons."

Knocking on the private separating window between them and the driver, Rick didn't take his gaze off of her. The window rolled down.

"Jerry...take us to the warehouse."

"Yes, sir."

The warehouse...this was beginning to feel like a suspense movie or detective TV show. Was he going to take her to the warehouse, tie her up and leave her for dead? What had Rick told her to do if she found herself in a situation she didn't feel comfortable in? Pray to God. She had no qualms about praying, but it seemed awkward for someone like Rick Delvante to suggest it so intently.

The limo stopped after what felt like hours as she tried not to stare across at her silent boss. She had nowhere else to look. The windows were tinted so heavily there was nothing to see besides their reflection in the glass.

Their driver opened the door and helped her out as Jack maneuvered silently to stand beside her. He unbuttoned his suitcoat and tossed it to the driver, nodding his head at her.

"Get her changed into something more appropriate for our trip. Get her geared up. I want her down here in twenty minutes to show me what she's got."

Confused, Tina looked around, thinking he was talking to his driver, until she heard a woman's voice behind her.

"Of course, sir."

Turning around, she was met by a stern-faced matronly woman. The pristine posture and hounds-toothed patterned skirt and jacket had Tina thinking she'd been a high school principal at an all-girls school. She tried smiling and holding out her hand in greeting, but the woman didn't budge, and she dropped her hand slowly to her side.

"Come with me."

Looking to Jack for acceptance, she had none. He'd already left, in the other direction.

"Hello, I'm Tina Joh—"

"We won't have time to exchange names or pleasantries. You have ten minutes to change and less time to be equipped before you leave."

The woman didn't stop walking. Tina followed in her wake, trying to take in the massive building they'd driven into to decipher what it held. Nothing from what she could see. Concrete walls and emptiness. Why have a warehouse if there was nothing there to keep?

In the far corner there was one box car crate large enough to hold a portable office perhaps. The woman led her there and opened the door, stepping inside and closing the door behind them. There was nothing in there, just more emptiness.

The crate rocked slightly. Tina held on to the metal side. Were they in an earthquake? Ms. Wet-Mop stood her ground like a captain aboard his ship, taking it all in as his men teetered around him on the rolling waves.

The motion stopped and the door opened. She was led out into a carpeted hallway. The shipping crate had been an elevator. A façade warehouse to house a—a what? Was this Jack Tabor's residence, like Mike's—just a cover-up?

The hallway appeared to go on forever. Very few doors lined the walls. They were the same elegant, colonial style doors she saw on most homes in Chevy Chase when Marilyn had been dating the congressman's son a few years back.

But they weren't homes and it wasn't a hotel—at least she didn't think it was a hotel.

"Here we are—we now have six minutes to get you dressed." The woman opened the door, and they walked into what appeared to be a military outlet of uniforms.

Rows upon rows of uniforms from various nations and military branches filled the room. Was this a recruit training facility?

"Put these on."

Tina was handed a set of military camouflage, complete with boots, ribbed tank top and cap...in her size.

"Quickly!"

There wasn't any dressing room around. She looked. The woman sighed in exasperation.

"Fine. I'll turn around. Trust me, where you are going, modesty will be the least of your worries."

* * *

Feeling out of place and more confused than ever, Tina, dressed like a new recruit, followed the woman from the wardrobe room to an underground arsenal. She could only gawk at the walls of various rifles, pistols, ugly looking knives and hand grenades.

"This is your pack. It has enough MRE's to see you for a full week, your first aid kit is well supplied with all the needed equipment. A tent, bedroll and various needful things will see you through in case of emergencies."

"MRE's?"

"Military rations...just add water."

The woman placed the eighty pound pack on her back. Tina instantly fell over...thank God on her back. But now she felt like a turtle turned upside down in the middle of the highway.

The elderly lady pulled her up—pack and all without any effort, whatsoever.

"You'll get used to the weight."

"So I'm good to go?" Tina asked hopefully.

"Of course not. We still have to get you your ammunition. You can't go into war without weapons."

* * *

She was going to war? What the hell?

Loaded down with enough metal to set off World War III, Tina was escorted further down the hallway. Struggling to keep herself upright and walking a straight line, she was suddenly pushed into a dark room, and the door shut heavily behind her.

The metallic click of a lock echoed around her.

Now was as good of a time as any to ask for God's help because she could only assume she was about to die.

Lights flickered around her like strobes, casting shadows of creatures and a darkened wooded landscape.

Okay God...are you there? I could really use your help. I don't know what the hell I'm—

Snarling interrupted her prayer and something heavy pounced on her, knocking her and her load of gear to the ground. She struggled with the human creature. Grabbing the knife she'd been supplied with, she attacked. The creature stilled, and she threw it off of her like a moth infested blanket.

But she wasn't out of the clear yet. On her back, she couldn't do anything. Helpless as that turtle lying in the middle of a highway, she waited. Her breathing heavy with adrenaline and fear, she could sense the danger around her...though this time there was no sound to warn her.

Lights flickered again, ever so briefly, and she sensed them more than saw them—a handful of attackers standing over her. Adrenaline turned to instant energy. She slid the ruck-sack from her arms and rolled just as the first one lunged, missing her by a hair. Kicking out with her legs, she managed to force two of her assailants down. The crack of shin bone and screams echoed around her.

The darkness had all her senses on alert. Suddenly she could smell her attackers, hear their nearly silent movements and feel the energy surrounding them. Hoisting her AK-47 strap over her shoulder, she pondered momentarily whether to stand or stay down. Compromising, she crouched low, her knife in her right hand at the ready. All hell broke loose.

Grabbed from behind by the arms and lifted off the floor, she kicked out—her foot coming in contact with solid chest. A loud grunt of pain followed. Bucking her head back, she rammed her skull into her holder's jaw with such force she swore it shattered. But it was enough for him to release her.

Tina stepped back into danger and another grabbed her by her left arm. Momentum started, she swung a wide arc and came back to plunge her knife in yet another assailants back. Her Karate moves came to mind and she half-blocked another with her hand, side stepped another attack and flipped him in the process. No longer thinking, Tina worked on pure instinct and motion. Each kick, jab or punch landing positively against her opponent.

She stopped, catching her breath and waiting for the next round of trouble. All of her senses were wired and on alert. It was amazing...the darkness no longer mattered.

The lights came on, flooding the room with radiance. She closed her eyes briefly to adjust the sudden dilation of her pupils. Bodies lay on the floor in a trail of where she'd been. The earlier attackers were beginning to move about, adjusting themselves, their bodies, as they began to heal.

Knife wounds suddenly sutured themselves together naturally. Bones snapped back into place with gruesome sounds... none of her attackers appeared phased by the ordeal.

Tina backed up, away from them. They were going to come in again and kill her.

A voice called out from the void. "Thank you all. I needed to see what she was capable of."

The group of young blond men waved to the voice and went on their way, some still limping or rubbing at their jaw.

A dark tinted shield of windows surrounded the arena she now stood in. Gazing up, she saw the side door to the watcher's box open and Jack Tabor walked out. Methodically stepping down the bleacher steps to where she stood, keeping his distance, he paced around her as if she were on display in a museum.

"So you're not a trained assassin?"

"No," she answered flatly. *Her a trained assassin, really?*

"Then perhaps you can tell me just what the hell you are?"

She was just a simple young woman. Why did he keep asking her that question?

CHAPTER SIX

RAMSTEIN AFB, GERMANY—

Mike Linder shouldered his rucksack and went for more supplies. The guards behind the desk scrutinized his government passport, orders and searched his bag for anything illegal. They asked him his date of birth, nationality and rank. He was still twenty-seven years old, same as he was at the time of his immortality, but his year of birth was 1988, not 1943. They would have him committed if he told them he was actually seventy-two years old.

Looking in the glass door as he made his way back out into the night air, he didn't look half bad for an old geezer. He wondered sometimes what he would actually look like if he had lived a normal life. It wasn't something to dwell on though. Not in his world.

Re-renting the BMW from the SIXT Rental Agency over at the Base Exchange for the next month, he hoped to make this assignment his last until Draylon and Marilyn's wedding. This assignment was a dead end. He hadn't been able to locate his European counterpart, Trenchfoot, to get a bearing on what was going down with the Vamiers in the area. His connections to finding anything out about Trenchfoot were dead ends. This wasn't the norm, and somehow he had a feeling that Rick was playing games with him.

Heading back over to Landstuhl, just across the airfield as a crow flies, he stayed at the Rosenhof Hotel & Restaurant, or the "Hof"as he'd named it. It was the only place he stayed when he was in this part of Germany. Sometimes he just came back for occasional visits.

* * *

The room was comfortably decorated with a low European, queen sized bed covered in folded duvet comforters and feather pillows, and a modern double sliding door armoire with enough room for five of his sea bag gear. A black leather sofa, large screen TV that only got BBC/CNN as an English channel and a marble and chrome desk for working from, made up his home for now.

He had his laptop set up, and using special codes and connections he had through his security company, he was able to tap into a lot of sources for whatever it was he needed, no matter where he was.

Trenchfoot, Code Name, Gold was his resource here. Gold was a rogue Vamier vampire, like himself, who ended up fighting the blood addiction and training himself to live on his own. He'd helped keep tabs on others and was the source of information to know what was shaking in the Western European sector.

The problem was finding the man. Gold was as valuable as the real stuff and twice as difficult to hunt down. The man never stayed in one place long enough to settle. A World War I soldier stationed in Belgium during the trench wars, Gold had been left for dead on the battle fields near Ypers until "given a second chance at life" by Vamier's immortal soldiers. They could never turn anyone without the victim'spermission...but when you were young and dying on a battlefield, some would dance with the devil for the chance to live. Unfortunately, they didn't understand the devil's dance card was always open and the cost was their soul for an eternity of thirst.

"Where are you old man?" Mike spoke aloud, not the first time in the past few weeks he'd been here. He let his fingers fly over the keyboard to fixate on a specific GPS signal that was the man's signature. Every contact had a homing device implanted into them by Livedel's biology team. Not to necessarily spy on what they were doing but to keep tabs on their health and nutritional intake. It was how they kept them supplied with the artificial hemoglobin or what they referred to as "transfusions." Most Vamiers couldn't stay in one place for long periods of time. They were immortal and needed to keep moving before suspicion set in among the natives.

Usually they were informed at headquarters if it was time for them to move on though, and they'd report in as soon as they had a new domicile.

Mike contacted the communications staff at Livedel. "This is Foxtrot, Three-Nine, reporting in from Landstuhl, Germany." He gave his serial number and call name to the switchboard operator.

"Go head, Foxtrot, Three-Nine."

"Anything new onGold-Charlie, Zero-Zero recently?"

"Negative, Foxtrot, Three-Nine."

"Still no positive signal on him?"

"I'm worried, Foxtrot. Trenchfoot is due for another transfusion and not having contact with him, not knowing where he is..."

"It's not like Goldto not call in. Is it possible he is in danger?" the operator asked worriedly

Mike loved the communications staff at Livedel headquarters. Most were widowed or empty nesters, middle aged women looking for a connection to a social work force again after raising families and being alone. They never lost their mothering skills, no matter that most of the characters they were helping were old enough to be their great-great ancestors.

"I'm sure he is fine, but I will let you know as soon as I hear something, HQ."

"Roger that, Foxtrot." She paused. "I still have you on locator now. You be safe out there."

"Yes, ma'am." He saluted, even though she couldn't see him over the mobile phone.

Yeah, no contact with Gold was not good. He was the only one in this area who might know about the wounded soldiers being brought in and turned. Mike just got more on his plate than he bargained for on this trip. First thing he had to do was find Gold...then he could find the wounded vets.

* * *

The shrimp flambé he'd had for dinner was wonderful, but the young woman he'd encountered at Christine's Cock-Pit Lounge was even more satisfying...for what he really needed. Mike had snuck a fifty into her purse while they were "necking"in the corner bar. He licked the sweet spot on her throat to close up the puncture wounds and tenderly entered her mind to wipe away all traces of what had transpired between them.

Satiated and mentally alert, he could now focus on the issues at hand. It was nearing eleven o'clock at night. He might get lucky checking out the hospital grounds for rogue Vamiers getting in and recruiting new vamps. None of this should be happening. According to Rick's speech a couple of months ago, after the Resurrection of Zamoxelis the Great, Aiden Vamier was going legit. Or at least trying to. You can't necessarily turn a villain into a saint after two thousand years. No, things might be a bit difficult to change by that time.

Mike made his way up the hillside from town to the base. The gates closed early, but he didn't need a stinking badge to get in. Being immortal had some advantages.

Still, he didn't like to go against his rule of breaking into something he wasn't assigned to break into. Even as a Navy SEAL he didn't like to go where no one had ordered him to unless it was a matter of life or death. This he constituted as a life or death situation...these wounded soldiers would lose more than their lives and dignity, they would lose their very souls.

The single floor hospital loomed stark white against the night. Security lights illuminated areas but left others in shadow. Great places for Vamiers to hide. The wings of the building spanned out like the letters "I" and "H" with nothing really connecting one with the other.

An end door was propped open, just inviting vampires in. He slipped in through the narrow fissure and looked around. A small office with a light on and computer monitor illuminated showed someone had just taken a break and would be returning soon. He needed to work fast.

Stealthily he made his way along the hallway until he heard the sounds of footsteps approaching. Hiding in the alcove between two patient rooms, he hoped the shadows hid him well enough. He could wipe anyone's mind but it was more of a hassle. He preferred stealth.

The two people moved past, talking to each other but stopped just out of his peripheral. Damn! Now he had to wait while they gossiped and hope they continued on soon. Looking behind him he noticed the patient's room was open. Smelling of antiseptic and sterilizing cleaner, the room lay dark and silent.

But Mike didn't need light. He had his super natural vision that creatures of the night needed in order to see their prey more clearly. The sound of beeping monitors and the whoosh of oxygen machines had him curious about the young patient.

Heavily bandaged from his head to the leg propped up on a pulley, Mike realized the other leg was missing beneath the covers. There was no formation. The kid was asleep, his breathing tube secured between his lips with surgical tape. His cheeks were red as if severely sunburned. Loose dressings mummified his right arm from shoulder to fingertips. The kid had suffered burns, lost his leg and was possibly concussed.

Shivers danced up Mike's spine. He wanted to leave, get the hell out of Dodge, but his feet wouldn't move. Blood raced through his veins and his heart prattled in his chest without a rhythm. Adrenaline was causing him to...he had to...get out.

He made his way back outside without being seen and sat in the darkness shaking. Every nerve in his body shook and nausea threatened to hurl itself out of him. Rocking back and forth, he repeated a mantra that Draylon had taught him.

"I'm alive...I have much to be thankful for...others need me...I need to fight for those who can't." The whispered words helped a bit, but for how long, he wasn't sure.

A dark shadow moved along the other wing across from him. Mike picked up his head, narrowing his vision on the entity. The form drifted in through the door as he had...but this wasn't him. Who would want to break into an Army Medical Ward where soldiers from the wars in the Middle East were sent after being wounded? The figure turned toward him, silver eyes flashing in the moonlight. Mike could smell the potent scent of bloodlust, a rogue Vamier vampire...waiting for the opportunity to turn an innocent, suffering soldier into an immortal basket case. This was his war. This was what he was hired for.

Silently creeping along the hallway and staying to the shadows, Mike followed the Vamier at a distance.

Passing nursing staff didn't notice either him or his nemesis checking out the various rooms. This hall didn't appear to have any patients in agony. There were no moans of pain or suffering. The silence unnerved him. It could mean many things, a comfortably sleeping soldier recovering from his assault, someone heavily induced by medication and not even conscious or the last case...the terminally or severely comatose men and women who'd been through the brunt of Hell and teetered on the edge of their mortal existence.

Glancing up at the paper nameplate on the side of the door, Mike wondered what Cpl. Timothy McCain suffered from. Slipping in silently behind the Vamier, he had time to stop any transfer of agreement between the young corporal and his enemy. Standing in the shadows, he knew when to strike and he waited.

Vamiers had to ask permission from their victims to be

turned...the promise of life was always offered and seldom refused. But no one was ever told the consequences of dealing with the devil. And Vamiers rarely elaborated.

Mike waited for the immortal to whisper his question. He had to wait for the words to be spoken aloud to the victim before he could act, otherwise he didn't have a case for attacking a Vamier and could be severely punished according to the Dacian laws. It was all based on fine-tuned timing. He peeked around the corner of the doorway to see what was taking the immortal so long to ask the question...sonofa—

His thought cut off mid curse as he saw the Vamier leaning over the unconscious Cpl. McCain and biting into his unfettered wrist, opening it up to take his victim's blood. Mike went into action, even though it was too late to change anything.

Reaching down, he took his silver blade from his combat boot and silently slit the throat of the immortal, turning his body to dust. It was expeditious and needed but...fuck! The transition wasn't complete. The victim needed to drink the blood of his maker or suffer death as a Shade...a soul trapped for eternity between Hell and something worse. He couldn't do that to the kid. The Vamier's head still lolled along on the floor, streams of blood still spritzing from the juggler. Picking it up, Mike placed the stream over the slightly parted lips of Cpl. McCain and rubbed the young man's throat until he swallowed what blood was going in.

When the blood stopped gushing, he threw the head down in disgust andit quickly deteriorated into dust. Looking around he picked up the young man in his arms, threw him over his shoulder and beat feet to get the hell out of there. As expected, as soon as the medical instrumentation was detached, alarms sounded up and down the hallway. The window was his only option. Breaking the glass with the beeping of the annoying IV stand, Mike threw himself and his burden out of the window just as footsteps rounded the corner of the room. He'd just "screwed the pooch" and life was about to become a real bitch.

* * *

Mike had to find someplace safe. He couldn't go back to the Rosenhof and endanger his friends there. The only place he could think of at this time of night was Franz von Sickingen's old ruins, Burg Nanstein. If he remembered correctly from previous trips, it was closed on Mondays so he'd have the ability to stay there for a good twenty-four hours at least.

Halfway up the steep, forested trail, Timothy McCain groaned. The kid was probably nauseous and bouncing around against his back wouldn't be helping matters. Finding one of the small, rustic benches, Mike carefully set his burden down. The kid lolled like a boneless mass until he could lean him up against the solid tree beside them.

"I'm sorry, buddy," Mike said as he examined the wounded soldier. "I had to do it. Anything else would have been unholy terror for you. Not that being immortal is a piece of joy, but at least you aren't trapped in an eternity of hell."

The young man groaned again, his brow furrowed in pain. Mike noticed the bite had stopped bleeding and was beginning to heal. His mortal wounds would heal within hours. But it would be the psychological shit of being turned that the kid would have to endure.

"You're gonna be okay...I promise. I've got your six, man." Mike didn't know if the kid even knew the naval aviator term for "having his back," hell he wasn't sure if the kid was Army or Marine. "I've got to get you to safety. But until we are safe, it's going to be a pain in the ass so bear with me."

Mike didn't even know if they were being followed. He didn't sense anyone around them, but that didn't mean the Vamiers were lying low. Picking up the corporal again, he carried him like a babe in his arms this time. He really didn't want the guy puking blood down his back.

Thinking about what he needed to do in the next twenty-four to forty-eight hours was mind boggling. He was basically on the lam until he could contact Dacia with the whole story. That was one of the problems, the story didn't make any sense. As much as he hated Vamiers, they lived by the ancient Dacian code. They'd never turned anyone without permission...well, he was an exception to the rule, but no one could figure out which Vamier had turned him back in Nam. His sire was definitely a mystery, even to Rick Delvante and his highly trained medical staff.

But the code of honor, never turn a mortal unless given permission, even if it is haphazardly asked, was a strict rule. It must be spoken aloud and the victim must be conscious enough to respond in kind—vocally, even if they weren't in their right mind at the time.

The Vamier back in the hospital ward, never asked, he just took. And in turn Mike had to kill him. But now, the only evidence was him stealing the wounded soldier and fleeing the scene. There would be some explaining to do once Rick and the

Dacian Council found out. And they would. By morning, every Dacian underground member would be on the lookout for him.

The Burg grounds were deserted. The tavern just outside the ruins shut down tight. The up-lights surrounding the fortress on the hill overlooking Landstuhl shone brightly and gave more than needed lighting to find his way around. His super sensitive eyes though didn't like the intense glare, and if he stood too close to them, Mike and the corporal would be crispy critters.

Timothy moaned again. The kid was coming around. Just a little bit longer until he could get him into the abandoned tunnels of the ruins. Finding the deepest cell, Mike lay the kid down. Taking off his camo jacket, he placed it under his head to give him some comfort. The terra cotta sandstone walls and floors were not the most comfortable, but they would have to do. Now he just had to wait, but from the blood tinged sweat beading up on Timothy's skin, they wouldn't have to wait long.

Less than an hour later the convulsions kicked in. It was the natural way a victim changed. The convulsions were the sign of the mortal soul leaving the body and renewing itself. Fever, chills, uncontrollable shaking, pain, they were all a part of the transition...and he didn't have a damn thing to give the kid to aid him in the physical and mental anguish to come. The transformation might kill him.

"I'm not going to lie to you, buddy. You're in for a wild ride." Mike tried to soothe the semi-conscious boy as the tremors began. The twitching of the fingers was the first sign. "If you make it through this without any drugs to counteract...I'll buy you a beer and call you a 'bad ass.'"

There wasn't much Mike could do. His main objective was

to make sure the kid didn't choke on his own blood and fluids as he vomited them. Otherwise it was just a process of waiting for the transformation and the first feeding, which wouldn't be for hours.

The agony of watching the kid who probably wasn't even twenty-one yet scream in agony as his body turned into a raging inferno of fever, the human anatomy trying to turn itself inside out as it repaired and replaced mortal for immortal parts and pieces, was almost too much for Mike to bear. But if the kid was surviving this, he could too.

He'd never been witness to an actual turning. Everyone involved with the immortal side of Livedel went through training documentaries on what to expect, but whenever he'd had to deal with a turning, it was handled by the secret medical team at Livedel, where medications and highly trained staff worked diligently to make the process as comfortable as possible. Even he had been one of the lucky ones and been found before the worst took place and he had to endure on his own.

Trying his damnedest to block out the horror, Mike closed his eyes and gritted his teeth against the screams that only brought back haunted memories of Vietnam. So many deaths. Tim's cries reminded him of his team members he'd lost. Their screams of pain and death as they were ambushed, echoing in his head.He'd never felt so damn helpless, lying there with his leg nearly severed after the grenade attack. The odd numbness and disorientation of being alive and unable to move, unable to help his friends, unable to be the leader he'd been chosen for. Shock. He'd passed out from the ordeal and woken up in a mobile surgical unit with Mama Kay and Doc Jon Johnston leaning over him.

The young corporal started to choke as he tried to scream past the pain.

Come on, Mike...get your chicken-shit ass off this ground and help him. You are his only source of help and you need to stop being the victim. It was forty-some-fuckin' years ago. Get a grip!

Slowly his conscience dictated enough motion to his brain to get him to scoot over to the kid. He turned him on his side, letting him spew out the bile and blood onto the dirt floor, letting the earth soak up the evidence of death. The worst was just about over...for now.

It was nearly an hour later when the young man finally stopped emptying his guts. The shaking would start up again, more violently than before. Cursing silently under his breath, Mike wrapped the hospital gowned kid up in his jacket and held him in his lap like a small child. Timothy was probably someone's kid brother off to make his mark in the world. Unfortunately, he would never be able to go home.

The tremors started and Mike hugged him tightly, whispering encouraging nonsense into Tim's, longish, military hair style. The kid probably hadn't had a hair cut in weeks. Marine's never let it get past peach fuzz, even if they were on their deathbed, so he assumed this kid was Army.

Another hour or two went by as he just held the kid. The tremors had ceased and a healing/resting period was in process. When Tim awoke, there wouldn't be a trace of his old wounds or human status. He'd be hungry for his first taste of blood—a tricky time at best. This was when the blood lust took place and if not properly appeased was a bitch to deal with and made many good men and women mad enough to go rogue...and he was one of the ones who had to kill them. Like rabid animals they only created death and destruction to those they encountered.

When Mike looked at his watch, time had passed. He'd even managed to get a few winks in as the kid slept. It was morning, but being as far underground and without windows as they were, only his watch knew the truth.

Timothy stirred from out of his dream-like state. His brows were pinched in uncertainty as if not sure he was supposed to wake or continue to sleep. Slowly his eyes opened up. Liquid silver, like mercury inside a glass orb, swirled in his irises. Confusion riddled his mind. Rick had been right...the newbies were so easy to read.

"It's about time you woke up, Corporal," Mike greeted with a gruffness in his voice.

The young man looked around. "Where...where am...I?" His voice squeaked and scratched like a thirteen year old boy's. How long it had been since he'd used it was anyone's guess at this point.

"Safe for now."

He looked down at the hospital gown beneath the large combat jacket. "What...what happened?"

Mike separated himself from the kid and gave him distance. He figured telling the corporal he was a vampire could wait for a minute or two. What he needed to know was why he wasn't in a hospital, or in combat. Remembering his ordeal nearly half a century ago, the first thing he did upon awaking was freak out because his company wasn't there and he was in a strange place he didn't remember.

"What was the last thing you remember?"

Closing his eyes, the kid tried to think. "We were in a convoy, taking supplies to a village..."

"Afghanistan?"

"No...Iraq. We'd just got done celebrating Saddam's execution at his palace and were sent to a nearby village..."

"Whoa! Back the truck up...Saddam was executed in December of 2006. That was nine years ago."

The kid didn't look old enough to be in his late twenties. He wasn't already immortal...was he?

"How old are you?"

"Nineteen."

"What year were you born?"

"1987."

This kid was actually twenty-eight years old and had been in the hospital for nine years? He needed to get some answers and he needed them...fast!

CHAPTER SEVEN

Tina forced herself to stay awake. Decked out as if she were going to Afghanistan for military combat, she sat uncomfortably trapped between two vampires that were also in the same camo gear. Across from her sat Jack Tabor, his eyes narrowed on her the whole trip, as if waiting for her to do something special.

Five months ago she'd never imagined being in this conundrum. Heck, four months ago she'd been safe in Mike's house, being watched over and...loved. Tina closed her eyes as the memory of the night she'd finally gotten him to surrender flooded her body with warmth. Tingling with sexual intensity at the way he'd tossed their wine goblets to the floor, picked her nearly naked body up in his arms and carried her to his bed had her aching. The image trailed off, like it always did when she thought of that night...the delicious things he'd done to her, his mouth, his hands, his...

"We'll be preparing for our jump soon," Jack broke into her thoughts as he commanded the group over the roar of the engines. "Ms. Johnston is with me. Meet up at our rendezvous site in two days. We go silent the second we land." He eyed each of the men sitting along the bench on the left side of the military airplane. He then sat forward and looked to the men to his left and right. "Understood?"

"Sir! Yes, Sir!"

Jump? What jump? He meant hop...as in hopping the next flight to wherever they were going? Right. Right?

A traffic light of sorts flashed a yellow "caution" light—or more like a prepare to jump light. The men sitting around her all got up and maneuvered single file to the back of the C-130 transport they were on. Jack gave a hand signal to the pilots in the cockpit and the tail began to open.

Oh dear God! She was going to have to jump, as in parachute! She hadn't been trained for this. Was this in the Shield Training and she just never made it that far?

Jack stood before her, strapping on his harness.

"I'm...I'm not...not...jumping—" she shook her head adamantly.

"I didn't say you were. I said you were with me."

While she still reeled from the shock and fear of jumping out of a perfectly safe plane, he grabbed hold of her harness she thought was just part of her gear strapped to her back and secured her to his front. Tina saw the co-pilot give them the thumbs up sign and felt herself being pulled backwards towards the rear ramp of the plane.

Screaming, pleading, she finally closed her eyes and silently prayed to God to give her strength to get through this ordeal. She could feel the air suck around them...she wasn't ready for this. Besides, she was being pulled backwards and couldn't see.

At last minute Jack turned with her in front.

Okay shit! Maybe backwards was better.

Her feet dangled off into nothing as Jack's feet toed the edge of the last piece of security. And then nothing but air.

Tina thought she was screaming but maybe it was all in her

mind. Jack's gloved hand covered her mouth briefly before they were jerked up by the billowing of the chute above them.

They went from free-falling to sudden stop as the chute deployed. Tina squealed in fear, keeping her eyes tightly shut so she didn't see death rush up to meet her. But then, she was lulled into security by Jack's body curving around her as he worked the lines to carry them to a safe landing.

"You're doing fine. But I need you to keep quiet as we land." Jack's deep husky voice tickled the outer shell of her ear.She leaned her head back into him, finally getting the hang of the feel of drifting downward like a feather. "Where are we landing? How can you see? It's pitch black out tonight."

"Trust me."

"It's not like I have a choice."

"You always have a choice—it's just knowing if the one you make is the best one for you."

Why did that sound more like a warning than the comfort she had hoped for?"

* * *

The landing went smoothly. Jack walked her through what she needed to do, and she realized she'd actually jumped from a plane.The rest of the crew were already dispersing into various directions as if on separate missions instead of as a team. Jack grabbed her by her upper arm and hurried her off to a dark tree line about fifty yards ahead of them.

He stopped, flashed a pinpoint red beam of light into the dense forest. A green light flashed twice. No bigger than a firefly and nearly as difficult to follow.

"This way," Jack said, dragging her along.

Tina had yet to catch her breath from landing in Dallas much less the long flight to wherever they were now. She was hungry and tired. Hopefully they'd find a nice hotel soon. She could do with a hot shower, a hot meal and a bed. Actually she didn't know if she'd make it to a hot meal and shower...a bed in a safe environment was all her body really craved. She was beyond hungry.

Stumbling through a bit of brush, they walked into pristine rows of pine trees. These trees were all trunk, the nearest limb appeared to be over twenty feet high. The rows looked like someone had planted them a perfect distance apart and the natural canopy of pine needled branches kept it even darker than imagined.

Jack seemed to know what direction he was heading in. Tina followed along blindly.

He stopped, she ran into his back. "Here, put these on?" He handed her a pair of black sunglasses. She put them on.

Strong lights illuminated the darkness, blinding her even with the fully tinted shades. At first she thought this was a movie set or a secret alien site. But it was only three utility vehicles, the size of Hummers that had made their way into the woods to meet them...or capture them.

A tall, lanky man dropped down from the middle vehicle. Tina noticed the bunched tension in Jack's shoulders at her side. His hands were rolled into fists, waiting for the first punch to be thrown. Were they trespassing? This scene didn't bode well.

The man stepped forward, towering over the both of them by a good six to eight inches, a lit cigar clenched between his teeth. He took a drag, lighting up the embers and exhaled between his teeth. His arms were across his chest in defiance. Rambo's dad perhaps?

"Who wrote '*In Flanders Fields*'?"

Why did that sound familiar? Was it a book...no, a poem she'd read when she was volunteering at the American Legion her junior year in high school. She'd been selling red poppies at the events leading up to Memorial Day that year. The poem was written by a man while serving in the trench wars of France and Belgium in World War I.

"John McCrae," Jack replied.

"What's the 'flower of remembrance'?"

"Poppies!" Tina blurted out.

Both men looked at her but didn't say a thing. She wanted to slink away at how they were eyeing her.

The man from the Hummer nodded his head and they were soon surrounded by the rest of the guerilla-like soldiers from the other vehicles. Her bag was removed from her back and one man began to pat her down.

"Hey! Whoa...watch the hands!"

She'd never been searched before, but something told her this guy was taking way too long. Tina could feel his heated breath on her neck. Had the asshole just inhaled her scent? That creeped her the hell out.

Now that she was unencumbered, she was able to move

around. Shoving her elbow back swiftly into the man's solar plexus, she heard the grunt and sensed him doubling over. Turning, she swung her combined fists into his back forcing him down onto the pine needle covered ground. Planting a booted foot on the back of his neck, near the base of his skull, all she had to do was put her full weight down and dislocate his spine from his brain.

Tina was forced back with an arm around her throat and both of her hands pinned behind her.

"That's quite a spit-fire you have there, Jack. Bright, beautiful—"

"She's not here for your pleasure, Trenchfoot," Jack replied to the leader.

"You were supposed to come alone after sending your troops out to scour the area. What's the idea?"

"I was instructed to bring her along."

"By whom?"

"Rick Delvante."

What? Rick had set her up all along. This was insane! She wasn't a trained Shield, and she had no business being here... wherever here was.

"Rick huh..." the man Jack referred to as Trenchfoot spoke around the cigar still in his teeth.

The two men stared each other down. There was definitely too much staring and eyeing each other up. Didn't anyone trust anyone else?

Jack gave a flourish, his arm pointing at her. “Let me introduce you to Tina Johnston, Code Name: *The Immortal’s Angel.*”

Trenchfoot stepped forward. “Well hell Angel, welcome to Germany.”

CHAPTER EIGHT

With the kid secure for now, Mike needed to keep an eye on the time. Beneath the ruins there was no sense of night or day and he was too exhausted to know. Other than his watch, he didn't have a whole lot to go on. Thank God he'd set it to German time when he landed in Ramstein.

Tim began to thrash about again. Hunger ate through the kid, but Mike didn't know how much more of his blood he'd be able to give. If it hadn't been for his meal at Christina's Cockpit Lounge, he'd be on the floor in a feverish fit by now, too.

He would wait. Giving into the kid's demands too soon would only cause him to want more. Mike needed to wean him off slowly, give him only enough to see to his basic needs. The groans of Tim's agony had his mind sinking slowly into the past. The screams and groans of his men as they lay dying...

No. He shook himself as if trying to stay awake. Awake and alert in the here and now. This wasn't Nam. There wasn't a damn thing he could do about the past. But the present didn't hold much hope. He needed to focus on something other than his own miserable existence.

The only bright light in his life lately had been Tina. He focused on her, the warmth she'd shared. A smile so brilliant it mimicked the sun. At times just looking at her his heart nearly burst with the love she tried to fill it with. He'd opened the valve to that fragile organ though and let her love seep out to puddle at his feet for him to step in...and wipe off like mud.

God you are an asshole, Linder. You could've been enjoying the sweetness of heaven and instead you might as well be in the bowels of hell.

Yeah, but where would the kid be? Would he have been in a better place or left for dead?

He didn't look much better off right now.

Mike scooted over to his young patient writhing around on the floor. The contortions alone were agony to watch as the hunger feasted on him. He would have to thank Momma Kay and Doc Jon when he saw them next time. They'd administered drugs while he'd gone through his transformation.

At least Tim hadn't begged to be fed. The kid was stronger than most. He wasn't sure what he would have done if he'd begged. But it wouldn't take long until the ache became so unbearable he might kill for nourishment.

Bringing his wrist to his mouth, Mike bit into his own artery, taking a chance that Tim didn't go ballistic upon smelling the blood. So far he hadn't, but there was always that first time. His mouth opened though, just like a baby bird waiting for food.

The steady flow of his blood trickled into Tim's mouth. He drank, nearly choking in the process. Tremors slowed and relief was quick but it wouldn't suffice for long. They didn't have time as a luxury. It would take days for the sickness to be weaned... months to learn to control it. Mike had less than—he looked at his watch—twelve hours before the ruins would be open to the public.

"Okay buddy, that's all I can give you for now." He licked the wound, sealing the torn flesh with his healing saliva. Helluva thing. Who would have thought spit had healing properties. He chuckled to himself, shaking his head. His mom would've loved knowing that—as many times as she'd used her spit and her thumb to wipe smudges off of his face as a boy.

Mike sobered. What he wouldn't do to have her do that again, one last time.

* * *

The night terrain held a special darkness all its own. If Tina could feel more uncomfortable with the men/creatures surrounding her, she didn't know how. Jack sat next to her and actually reached over to hold her hand. But he really hadn't said much to her since the reveal of her "Code Name." She'd turned to him for answers back in the forest, but he shook his head, signaling this wasn't the time to discuss anything. He wasn't kidding. No one said a single word, and she wasn't about to be the one to break the silence.

But so many questions were dive bombing her brain. Why did she have a code name and why had Rick ratted her out? She was supposed to be undercover, according to him. Was Delvante playing her for a fool? Or just playing with her life? She wished she could contact Marilyn and talk to her about her father—maybe she had answers or could get them.

And then she thought of Mike. Did he have any clue where she was or what was going on? What had he thought when she didn't show up for his classes? Had Rick told him she was on a "special assignment"? Or had the man told him anything at all? Did anyone know where she was? She knew her parents were probably informed by now. They probably had first-hand knowledge of her activities since Marilyn came back to the States from her trip to Europe. Since then things had turned a bit weird. And she'd thought her parents wouldn't understand the fact her friend was immortal. Or that she'd been in danger from a group of bloodthirsty vampires she'd worked for at the blood bank. Ha! They knew. They knew everything.

When she'd been with Mike, they'd been informed that she was being protected and taken care of. They knew she'd had an interest in her "protector."She should've known something was up when her parents didn't ask questions—when they'd been around. Now she knew. He was one of Rick's guys. They would trust him. But why had she trusted him? And now...and now... she didn't know anything.

Tina felt her chest tighten as she stared out into the darkness. It appeared like a foreign entity to her, surrounding her and yet not coming any closer than her peripheral sight. As if it too didn't know what to make of her. Alone. Never had she encountered being alone, even among those surrounding her.

Tears fell. She could sense them before they pooled in her eyes. Each drop landing heavily on the ridge of her uniformed chest.

Jack grasped her chin in a delicate but firm grip. He turned her face towards his, those black obsidian eyes full of amazement and wonder. His finger traced the trail of moisture up her cheek to her lash line. A tender gesture to wipe away her tears.

Pulling his finger away from her face slowly, Tina looked at the tip of his finger where the drop of moisture should be. It wasn't moisture but a teardrop shaped crystal.

Shock had her raise her trembling hand to her cheek to pull

another small gem away. She looked down at her top. Five perfectly formed teardrop stones lay pooled in the divot of her shirt near the buttons. Gathering them in her palm, she studied them in the dim light of the automobile.

Gaping up at Jack, she expected some sort of answer. Was it her imagination or did the two men sitting across from her try to scoot further away from her? Why wasn't Jack? No, he sat there with a smug, satisfied grin on his face. The firm line of his lips curved ever so slightly up at the corners. Tina didn't think she'd seen him smile before.

"Well, well...that explains a lot. If what the legends say are true, you really are theImmortal's Angel."

* * *

Shaking and wanting answers to the craziness that was happening to her, Tina had every intention to write this all off as some terrible dream. But the fantasy wasn't ending with a pinch or her silent demands to wake up. Not even the jarring of back road potholes could wake her.

Jack had taken her teardrops and placed them carefully in the front pocket of his gear vest without a word or further explanation. She had no idea even though he'd appeared pleased at the thought.

She wasn't immortal. She was a normal human being.

Their caravan stopped. They were outside a military looking facility waiting for access onto the site. Within moments all three Jeeps were parked in a remote parking lot surrounded by more darkness.

"Jack, I need Immortal's Angel with me," Trenchfoot leaned

into their Jeep.

"No. She's not going anywhere unless I'm with her."

Trenchfoot looked around the darkened area as if contemplating the situation. "Okay. But I need her...if what Rick says is true. She'll be a true asset."

Tina was tired of all of this bull. No one was telling her anything or talking to her. Instead they were talking about her as if she weren't there, in riddles.

"Wait!" She sat back in her seat, her arms crossed staunchly across her chest. "I'm not going anywhere with anyone until I at least get some answers."

"We don't have time for answers—not right now." Trenchfoot's growling command gentled a bit, as if remembering he was talking to a woman, not one of his immortal creatures.

"Then I'm not going. Find yourself another 'Immortal's Angel.'"

"We can't. You are the only one," the man stated impatiently.

Jack turned to her. "Tina, we need your help. Rick told me he was sending me the Immortal's Angel—someone who could help out some of the wounded soldiers who were turned but not all the way. They were turned but never given immortality—they're trapped in a world somewhere between this world and the next. Only theImmortal's Angel can help them."

She knew that but why was she with these people? What was their purpose? Were they trying to form their own clan like Rick was afraid they might be?

The gentle pleading and hope of understanding in his eyes tugged on Tina's sensitive heartstrings. Wounded warriors trapped between life and death. She was their only hope?

Was this it? Was this what all of her training was leading to?

"Just be there." Jack looked from her to Trenchfoot. "I don't think we know what will happen. Rick said only theImmortal's Angel could ease their pain and suffering."

She pondered the situation. She'd been instructed on how to use her instincts but was this the right place and time? Rick Delvante hadn't told her to do this exactly. Not now.

"We don't have a lot of time. Dawn is approaching in less than fourhours. We need to move now," Trenchfoot broke into her thoughts.

Tina nodded her decision. There were wounded, half immortal soldiers. She had to help them.

Sticking to the shadows around them, they made their way across the open field to a single floor building. One wing of the building had an emergency door propped open just enough to let someone in. They were met by a woman in a medical coat. Checking the closest room, she pulled them all in.

"We had a bit of an issue tonight, Gold," she rushed to tell them, holding up her hand so no one interrupted her. "One of the soldiers that has been here for many years was taken. One of your men, trying to turn him, was murdered."

"Keating? I sent him here to turn the young corporal. Who killed him?"

"I don't know. All we know is someone came in during the

change of shift, must have seen Keating trying to turn Timothy and cut his head off. We found two piles of ash and a trail of blood splatter. The attacker crashed through the window when the I.V. alarm sounded and made off with Timothy."

Trenchfoot cursed and paced the floor. "Take me to the room. Let me see if I can find any clues the attacker may have left." He turned to Jack. "Take Tina to the other wounded. Let's see if she can do anything with her powers."

"Let's go." Jack took her by the arm. "You're their only hope, Tina."

Having Jack lead her out, why did she suddenly feel like Obi Wan Kenobi?

* * *

Tina's first patient was missing both of his legs. One at the hip and the other at his knee. He lay there so still, as if in death, but the closer she approached him, she could sense his life essence still lingering...weary but still hanging on.

As if by instinct she walked to his side, the pull of his life energy strong. She placed her left hand on his forehead and the right on his chest, over his heart. Closing her eyes, Tina was swept away into a haze filled darkness, but there was illuminating light behind her.

The young man sat on an outcrop of darkness that had formed a seat. There was nothing for him to see or do. He was alone, bent over. He looked up as she approached, shielding his eyes from the brightness.

"Are you an angel?"

She should tell him the truth. “No...I’m just a woman.”

“You must be an angel. There’s no one else here.” He looked down at his whole self for what might’ve been the first time in a long while. “I thought I’d lost my legs. I guess I haven’t. That’s a relief. I can’t wait to get back home and play football with the guys.”

“You didn’t dream it. You did lose your legs. It’s only here that you have them.”

She couldn’t stop being truthful with this young man. The words flowed out of her mouth without conscious thought or control.

He grimaced. “Where’s here?”

“It’s a waystation. When you are ready, you can make your decision...and I will help you pass.”

“I have the opportunity to live but without my legs?”

“Yes. The life won’t be yours though. You will be an immortal being, forced to live off of the blood of man. It is a life many choose but few survive. There is only darkness, and you will have no contact with your former family and friends,” she offered automatically.

He shook his head. “That’s no life...what is my other option?”

“I can light your way to the doorway of salvation. You won’t ever be alone in the dark again.”

He nodded. Tina held out her hand and he took ahold of it. Leading him into the darkness, the light followed them so it was never really dark. But it was empty. Tina found the door and easily opened it. Before them was a green field, park and laughing families. Someone tossed a football at him. He caught it. A grin plastered on his face. He looked at her, kissed her cheek quickly.

"You are an angel. Thanks."

And he went to join in the game.

Tina sped back into reality. Exhaustion and joy mingled as she sat at the bedside of the young soldier. He was gone. His life energy no longer surrounded her. His forehead was cold and the beat beneath her hand was no more. She cried. Not in sadness, but in joy, for he'd found his way.

Jack's hand gently rested on her shoulder.

She opened her eyes to see her tears had turned into a rainbow of crystals piled beside the empty body belonging to the peaceful soul *she* had helped move on.

Jack helped her to stand. Thankful for his support, she smiled wearily up at him.

"So I am an angel."

Kissing the crown of her head, Jack whispered, "I know you are."

Trenchfoot burst into the room. "No time for lovey-dovey crap...I know who killed Keating, and I think I might know where to find him."

CHAPTER NINE

Dawn was mere hours away. Mike needed to figure out a safe place to go. Nothing came to mind. If he could only find Trenchfoot, he'd be able to find them sanctuary. But if no one had heard from him in a while, the man could be anywhere in the world. Rick would have a cow. No one left an area without reporting in to Delvante. It was a matter of safety and protocol. But if Livedel's satellite communications systems weren't picking up his tracks...damn! Those were his satellites they'd launched for security protocol. He hadn't heard of any communication issues lately.

The kid was at least resting peacefully after his last feeding. Mike wondered if he had any blood left in him. The weakness he felt could be just the need to sleep, but adding a depleted iron level made for one messed up vampire.

Drifting in and out of sleep didn't help his timing issues. It was difficult to make plans when you had nothing to go on but brainstorming. And his brain was so sluggish right now, he didn't even think he could protect himself, much less the kid.

A scurry of noise roused him like a dose of caffeine straight in the arm. He listened, waiting in the entrance to the dark hallowed out room. Was it an animal lost in the labyrinth of the ruins? Could it be one of the guides doing an early check? He looked at his watch, 0432, no guide would be up this soon on a Tuesday morning.

Pulling his knife he would either have blood of a rodent to keep him semi-alert for a while or attack someone to keep safe.

Either way he'd have a meal.

The noise grew louder. If it was an animal, it was huge.

Whispered voices. He couldn't quite make them out. Shit! This didn't bode well.

"Foxtrot if that's you, stand down."

Only one person knew his secret call sign besides HQ. The one person he'd been looking for.

"Gold is that you, man?"

"It's me."

Trenchfoot came around the corner and they embraced like long lost brothers.

"Where've you been? HQ didn't have a trace on you...Who's with you?"

"Whoa. Slow down son." Trenchfoot studied him. "You look like Hell."

"Thanks. I feel like it, too."

They looked over at the sleeping figure on the ground. "How's the young corporal?"

"Weak. The turning is draining him—" Mike scratched his head. "How do you know the corporal? Did you knowthe kid was wounded over eight years ago?"

"I know. It's okay. We'll explain everything once we get you and Tim out of here." He looked at his watch. "We haven't got much time. Night time is running out."

"I was just sitting here wondering where to go." A scrabbling of dirt sounded from out in the corridor. Mike went on alert. "Who's with you?"

Trenchfoot called over his shoulder. "It's safe. You all can come out. Might need your help, Angel."

All his senses came on full alert. He didn't know anyone with a code name, Angel.Trenchfoot always worked alone. The man didn't like to be tied down.

The sight that met him coming around the doorway stopped his heart briefly.

"Tina?"

"Mike!"

He wasn't sure if she sounded excited or shocked. But he was both. What the hell was she doing in Germany?

"You two know each other?

On the most intimate of terms.

"What's she doing here, Gold?"

"She's here with me."

Mike turned to see the other man in the doorway. If seeing Tina was a shock to his system, the man standing before him had him wanting to flat line. He shook his head slowly, trying to absorb the vision before him. No. It couldn't be.

"Jo...Jo...Johnny?"

"Hello Mike."

* * *

Relieved there were others around her, Tina didn't know what to think. There was Mike. What was he doing here? What was going on, really? And why was Mike so shocked by seeing Jack Tabor?

Wondering what to do, she looked to Trenchfoot for a sign. He appeared to be as confused as she was. Pointedly looking at his watch, he gave her a nod to check on the man on the floor.

After a few moments of focusing on the sleeping victim, her instincts told her he'd already passed the three-quarter mark of the turning process. He only had twooptions now, immortality or a vampire's death.

Still Mike and Jack stared at each other. Neither saying another word. Tina could tell Mike was stunned but reading Jack was more difficult.

"Come on guys. Snap out of it!" Trenchfoot commanded as he bent to hoist the dead weight of the infant vampire off the floor and over his shoulder. "We've got too much to do before sunrise and having a silent pissing contest as to who can stare the longest isn't in our repertoire."

Tina stroked Mike's arm lightly to gently get his attention. Even with the slight connection, she could feel the radiating tension and a deep seeded pain keeping his frame rigid and uncompromising.

"Mike...we need to leave. It's okay." She looked between Mike and Jack. "Jack, tell him it's okay."

He shook his head. "I can't tell him what I don't know." Jack's voice rasped on a hint of emotion. "I don't know if anything will be okay, ever again."

* * *

The quiet ride to the border of Luxembourg and Germany, trying to stay ahead of the sunrise, proved to be full of as much angst and mystery as the reason she was here in the first place. Something or someone had to give, and Tina was afraid it would be her. She sat in the middle seat, Timothy's head resting in her lap as she smoothed his hair back and comforted the soul within by her touch.

An angel? Was she really such a creature? How had she become one and on whose divine authority made it so? TheImmortal's Angel, a title derived from some ancient tome. Rick Delvante had a lot of explaining to do. She wanted answers from him but wasn't sure if she could ask him without wanting to throttle the immortal clan leader until his brain rattled.

Marilyn had dealt with her father and all the secrets only a few months ago, and now she was anything but the woman she'd been when they'd left college in Towson. Human, immortal, a creature of legend and folklore? What were they really, and why were they both thrust into this unbelievable reality that no one would ever believe?

The more she thought, the more frustrated she became. Her patient moaned and twitched beneath her hand. She was transferring her pain and emotions to him. He didn't need that right now. No one needed that. She quieted her thoughts and focused on calming him with soothing energy.

Trenchfoot's home was a small fortress. A preserved ruin from the bombings of World War II. Like Mike's house, it was only a façade to cover an even more intricate system of underground rooms and tunnels to keep their kind hidden and confuse any possible poachers.

Once they settled Tim down and hooked him up to an I.V. of hemoglobin, the four of them sat down in the cavernous underground den, an actual room carved out of a large underground grotto. Trunks of stalagmites and stalactites formed curtained walls, other formations had been designed either naturally or manmade to make up seating and ambiance.

Creeks and shallow rivers intertwined with the formations, making it appear like lakeside property. Trenchfoot had placed various colored lights within the water to reflect the cave and made it look thousands of feet deep.

"Well hell, this is going to be a long ass morning!" Trenchfoot stated as he finished his glass of hemoglobin.

Mike had downed two bags, refreshing his own need and the extra he'd lost from helping Tim turn. Jack drank his but sipped more than took it as nourishment. Maybe he didn't need as much. He hadn't been drained or denied for days. Still, Tina realized it made him so different from either Mike or Trenchfoot.

"Are you two going to talk at all or just stare at each other? Are you fighting over this girl?"

Silence.

"It would be the only thing that made sense with you two right now." Trenchfoot waved his hand at them. "Aw...I'm not sitting around waiting for you two to figure things out. I'm going to bed."

Tina wasn't going to have any of it. Nobody seemed to care about her. Not that she was hurt, but she was in this conundrum, too. Had been since Rick sent her to Dallas to be made into G.I. Jane and flown over Germany to be dropped like some unassuming bomb. Well she was about to blow and God help them when she did.

"No one is going anywhere! Not until I get some answers."

"Shit! Angel, can't it wait until nightfall? I'm bushed." Trenchfoot pulled at his moustache.

"No, it can't wait." She walked over between the two men glaring across a makeshift coffee table. "You two, snap out of it. Neither one of you are getting out of this. I should be the one brooding and pissed."

Once she had everyone's attention she laid into them.

"I've been lied to, set up and left in the dark this whole mission. I won't stand for it anymore..."

"Tina—" Jack began.

"No. Shut up...shut the hell up. This is my turn to vent. Then you can say whatever you want, but everyone is going to listen to me and answer some questions...and answer them straight, no bullshit or crappy riddled answers. Understood?" She looked at each man individually.

She had Mike, her beloved Mike, looking like he just came off the battle grounds, shell-shocked. Jack, as pristine as a financial executive even in camouflage. And Trenchfoot, a grizzled older man with a mustache to match the early 1900's era he'd came from. What a group.

"Now. You," she pointed at Jack. "You haven't been truthful with me from the beginning. I want every last detail about my mission. Why did Rick send me to work for you...really?"

Jack sighed. "He said he was sending me theImmortal's Angel."

"That's not the assignment he gave me." But she wasn't about to let anyone know what it was.

She looked directly at Trenchfoot who nodded solemnly. There was so much to this story and that nod showed her they were all a part of it.

Jack continued, "About six months ago I received messages from some of my European connections that there was a new batch of rogue Vamiers infiltrating parts of Germany and surrounding countries to the south and west. I had my operatives look into the possibilities of a correlation. They put me in touch with Trenchfoot." Jack nodded back at the older man.

Trenchfoot took it from there. "I'd been hearing rumors of soldiers coming in from the Middle East sharing the same conditions as rogue Vamiers. Being offered eternal life in exchange for their souls on the battlefield—except the victims weren't given a say. They were being turned against the clan laws. They were picked up by medivacs and taken to Landstuhl as wounded soldiers. I have connections at the Army hospital where I'm able to provide a separate ward for those specific soldiers. In the meantime, I needed someone who could send me troops to locate any other rogue vampires wandering about Germany, Switzerland, Austria, Luxembourg and France. So I contacted Jack Tabor."

"And what exactly is your part in this?"

"I've been supplying vampire soldiers, my own breed, to help find the rogues. Most of the ones we've found are too far gone...we put them out of their misery."

"Isn't that what Rick Delvante does? Why are you involved with it?" Tina wasn't aware anyone but Rick had the control to hunt and kill rogues.

Jack didn't speak for a moment but looked expectantly at Mike who sat quietly brooding, his jaw as tight as the muscles bunched in his folded arms.

"For years, until recently even, I never knew of the Delvante or Vamier clans. I lived in a convenient world, thinking I was my own master of fate. I was in control...I said who lived and who lived immortally. It took me over a decade to fight my own addiction and to learn from it. Once I did, I set my sights on returning to the real world." He looked at Mike again before going on.

"I made mistakes, not knowing what I truly was or that my former self was listed as Missing In Action...to this day, along with the rest of my squad. Once I did know, I realized I had to create a new life, a new identity and do something that would keep me financially secure for centuries to come. Rick Delvante found me—about two years ago. He'd been keeping tabs on me and my business. When he came out to meet me in person, I was given the information and warned against the violations I'd already committed. He forbid me to turn anymore and set me to create a haven for those willing to abide by the Delvante Rules governed by the Ancient Dacian Leaders."

"So you are now part of the Delvante Clan?" Tina asked.

"Unofficially, yes. But I still hold my own control over my clan. We are 'partners' if you will."

"And what am I? Why did you send for me?"

"I didn't send for you. As I said, I was informed the only one who could help the men and women soldiers who were suffering from rogue Vamiers turning them was the Immortal's Angel."

Were there more of these Angels around? "How many of them are there?"

"As far as Rick knows...one. You."

Mike stood up. "And just what is theImmortal's Angel?" He looked around at both men and her.

Tina was flabbergasted. It was the first words he'd said since they'd left the ruins in Landstuhl. But she couldn't answer his question.

"Rick has a better grasp on what they are," Trenchfoot spoke up as Jack appeared afraid to speak. "But from what I've been told, the Immortal's Angel is chosen by Zamoxelis himself to be a comforting entity for his immortal warriors in their time of need."

Jack looked at her. "Rick sent you to help me. He knew you could ease the troubled souls of the wounded, partially turned soldiers we'd found."

"What about Tim?" Mike asked with a snarl. "Did you know he's been in a coma for over eight years? What the hell happened to him?"

Trenchfoot sighed. “He was one of the first one’s I encountered. He’d been turned but I hadn’t known it. I killed his maker thinking he was rogue...he disintegrated into ash before the transformation was complete. I had him set up in a private ward as the first patient of many, leaving him as a Shade until I could find someone with the same blood-type as his maker.”

“Keating,” Jack stated.

Trenchfoot nodded sadly. “Unfortunately, a lack of communication somewhere along the way had Mike kill him the other night.”

“Speaking of which, why are you here in Germany, Foxtrot?”

“Rick sent me. Said there was a band of rogue Vamiers turning the military wounded at Landstuhl. He told me he wanted it stopped. He’d lost communication with you and figured he could send me to kill two birds with one stone. My job has always been simple, find a rogue Vamier and kill it, no questions asked.”

Jack spoke up. “It’s not always their fault. They can’t control themselves. I’m trying to rehabilitate the ones who are strong enough to fight. I had a hard battle to fight myself, but I did it and so can they.”

The response didn’t come. The standoffwas at hand. Tina knew these two men knew each other—had they been former enemies or what?

Mike’s voice cracked. “What happened to you, Johnny? Where were you that night we were ambushed?”

Silence. Jack looked away, his back to Mike, as he stared out over the red colored reflective pool.

"I led the squad in, wanting to prove I could lead a group of men, too. When we got there, the place was already torn apart. Only a few bodies remained. I had my men search the perimeter of the compound. I heard the sounds of animals attacking and screams from some of my men. I went to search for them and this creature, a rogue Vamier latched onto my neck and forced blood down my throat. I lay there, dazed and delirious."

He stopped, his shoulders slumping, but he never turned around. "I vaguely remember you and the rest of the squad coming in to investigate. You saw the carnage as did a group of Charlie's approaching. Seeing the destruction, and assuming the Americans had destroyed the compound, they launched grenades and fired into the squad. I saw you, Mike. I heard you give the orders, I heard the cries of my fellow teammates as they were blasted into bits. Then I saw the burst of light that took you out. But you weren't dead...you crawled a few feet with your leg dangling by a tendon. You turned over, waiting for death..."

Tina felt the sting in her eyes. She almost couldn't watch but she did. Mike sat heavily on the cushion topped rock formation. His hands covering his face, shaking his head in disbelief, he seemed to know what was coming.

"...your blood...I craved it like I was starving. Man, you looked like a banquet. I just wanted a little...you asked me to look after Mom...Mike...shit...I can't say it, Mike...don't make me say it."

"What did you do, Johnny?" Mike's words were quiet and anything but controlled.

"Mike...please...I didn't mean to...I'm sorry..."

"What did you do?"

Tina nearly jumped out of her skin at the harsh command from Mike. He was holding onto his control by a fine thread of inner peace.

"Tell me!" Mike bellowed as he stormed across the distance separating them. He spun Jack around to face him.

"I turned you."

CHAPTER TEN

The drips of moisture from the grotto echoed in the silence. Not even a breath could be heard. Mike looked at his friend. So much the same yet so different. His fingers loosened on Jack's arm.

"I didn't mean to, Mike. I didn't know what came over me...I had no control...I was hungry...so hungry..." Jack sobbed openly. "I didn't know what would happen. I don't know what had happened to me."

Mike backed away, unsure of how he was feeling, cold, panic, confusion, pain so deep it made his heart ache. For those who said "the truth would set you free," they were full of shit. He'd been so shocked to see his buddy alive and well a few hours ago...the first time in over forty years. And now, to know he was the one who'd turned him? His mind struggled to take it all in.

Tina stroked his back. A supporting gesture from her. The radiation of her warmth met his heart, releasing the ache as if by magic. Her other hand held onto his arm. God it was good to feel her touch again. Her tiny fingers were a balm, absorbing the pain he felt so deeply. She leaned her head onto his shoulder.

The sound of tiny pebbles hitting the rocky formation beneath their feet had him looking down. Ruby red jewels the size of drops of blood speckled the ground.

"What the...?"

He bent to pick them up as a few more hit the ground. Had Tina dropped them? Squatting, examining the delicate jewels in his palm, he turned to look up at her.

Blood red tears streaked across her porcelain cheeks, dropping into hardened crystals at their feet.

Sonofabitch!

Mike stood up and examined Tina's face. She tried like hell to smile but there was pain, so much pain etched into her features. Not a word, not a sniffle or sob...just tears and anguish pouring from her eyes like bloody tears that turned to gems.

Her body convulsed as if it were trying to turn inside out.

Picking her up, he held her as much as he could until he could place her on the makeshift sofa cushions. Kneeling beside her, he could feel the presence of the other two men nearby. His animal instincts activated and he snapped at them, hissing and showing his fangs. They responded in kind but backed away.

This isn't the time to go vamp on her, Linder. His consciencewarned him, but it didn't stop him from feeling protective of his Tina.

She's not yours, man. You gave up that right a while ago.

Tina went into a fetal position, telling him her pain was intense. Why wasn't she crying, screaming...anything?

"Come on, baby. Cry. Make a sound...something." He tried to soothe her.

"She can't, Mike," Trenchfoot said from behind him.

"Why the hell not?"

"She's theImmortal's Angel. According to legend, she just absorbs pain from her patients. Her body is dealing with it the best it can."

What the hell was he talking about? She wasn't immortal. And he definitely didn't want her absorbing his pain. *He* was barely strong enough to absorb it. Why was she even here? Rick sent her here...or to Johnny, Jack whatever the hell he called himself now.

"Get Rick on the phone, I want to talk to him."

The old man better have some answers or he was heading back to Maryland to roast him on a spit.

* * *

The visions would not go away. The more she tried to erase them from her mind, the more they came back to bombard her. Tina felt the pain, suffered it in silence. Her body screamed, fighting with her to release the emotional trauma.

She was lying on her back, bombs and screams of men all around her. Physical pain ripped through her body. She turned to look behind her and saw her leg nearly severed. Blood and material shredded together, exposing bone and muscle. Crawling, inching her way along the ground by her fingers, she made it to the edge of the jungle and flipped over onto her back. She didn't want to die with her face in the dirt. She wanted to look up at Heaven.

Nobody could suffer to this extent. Why was she? Where was she? This wasn't her. It was but only in her mind. She was viewing a different time, a different place, through someone else's terror filled eyes.

There was a man leaning over her. Familiar but not.

Johnny…it's you…you're alive…take care of Mom…

More agony, this time like a thousand needles tearing into her throat. Fire…blood, red haze…and darkness.

God, help me, she pleaded.

Her body stilled. No more pain. The vision left but didn't leave her with the sense of peace she hoped for.

Opening her eyes, she found Mike leaning over her, stroking her hair. A weak smile was plastered on his face, but his eyes betrayed his concern.

"Hey," his voice croaked out.

Never had she seen him appear so tender. She reached out and touched his cheek. He turned his head, kissing her palm reverently.

"Is she okay?"

Tina looked away, seeing the face she'd seen only moments ago in her dream. The one who'd been leaning over her. Jack Tabor.

"It was you," she said. "You attacked me out there in the jungle…you're Johnny."

She sat up. Both men looked at one another with confusion, and then back at her.

"That wasn't me…that was you, Mike. You were lying on the ground, your leg severely injured…you crawled on your belly to the edge of the compound and rolled over, waiting for death…" her voice trailed off.

"You saw all of that?" Mike asked cautiously.

"Saw it, lived it, felt your pain..."

Mike winced and rubbed his face. He began to pace and curse with every step. The words he uttered weren't a comfort.

Trenchfoot walked back into the room. "I have Rick on the line. Did you still want to talk to him?"

"Damn right I want to talk to him. Put him on speaker," Mike snarled mid-curse, yanking the phone from Trenchfoot's hand. He paced back towards Tina.

She worried about what Rick might do with Mike's angry disposition. She hoped he would cool down a bit before he went too far.

"You want to explain the shit you have going on, Old Man?" He punctuated with his index finger as he spoke over the phone. "What did you do to Tina?"

"I didn't do anything to her, Mike." Rick's voice echoed clearly off the stone walls.

"You sent her here for a reason. I want to know why. And Jack Tabor...really. You expect me to believe you had nothing to do with him being here, bringing Tina with him?" Mike fought to control his anger. "What. Is. This. About. Rick?" Each word enunciated sharply to accent the anger behind it.

"Things are changing in our world, Mike," Rick said.

"Stop! Just stop with the riddles. I want straight answers," Mike answered back.

"Fine, you want straight answers? I'll give it to you straight...

the gods are pissed and if we don't make things right, none of us will be alive to do a damn thing about it...and I'm not talking about just us as in 'immortals,' I'm talking about mankind as we know it."

"What gods? The Dacian gods?"

"The Dacian gods, the Hindu gods, Greek gods, Christian god...name any religion and their god or gods are really at the end of their ropes with us. We've caused wars, famine, climate changes, desecrated the lands they gave us, hunted to near extinction the very creatures they put on this earth for us...all in the name of greed, power and vice."

They all looked at each other with knitted brows. Should they deny what Rick was saying? This all seemed a bit far-fetched.

"And what are we supposed to do about it?" Jack spoke up.

It took a while for Rick to answer as he perhaps gathered his thoughts.

"There are those of you who are on the right page to building a better world. Jack, you came forth to help the rogue Vamiers find the opportunity for peace they need. The gods approve. Yes Mike, I sent you on the same mission to make amends and team up to break the cycle of anger and resentment from years of wondering where your friend was, if you had killed him..."

Jack looked at Mike expectantly. "You thought you killed me?"

Mike waved his question away. "That doesn't answer my question about Tina. What the hell did you do to her?"

“Nothing that wasn’t supposed to happen at the right time and place.”

“What’s that mean exactly?” Mike looked at her.

Rick sighed. “Each of us is here on this earth for a reason. Sometimes we are aware of what it is our task is and other times, we aren’t. Tina was placed here by the Dacian gods to help rebuild the immortal clans. She was born theImmortal’s Angel for when the gods deemed it time for her to make her presence known.”

“Why wasn’t I told? Do my parents know?” Tina spoke up.

The pause of silence had them all waiting, wondering if they’d been disconnected.

“Your parents know. They’ve known since they tried to conceive all those years ago. I’ve known your parents for a long time, Tina. They came to me to get in contact with someone who could help them have a child.”

“And?” Tina was almost afraid to ask. She’d never known. Her parents never talked about their life before her.

“They were given a blessing by the goddess of fertility, Sanziana herself—in exchange for your task when you were of age.”

“My task? What exactly is my task?” Her voice shook with uncertainty.

“You are the only one who can soothe and guide the poor souls bound to an eternity of suffering by having been turned rogue. You absorb their suffering so they can move on in death or take their place in immortal society. You are not only an angel of mercy but an angel of death. I’m sorry for all the deception,

Tina. All of you, I'm sorry. Things are definitely happening fast and there was no way to prepare for it. I had to play my cards close to my chest until I knew for sure who was on our side. It's not an easy task being the leader of the immortal world."

* * *

Did any of them really believe what Rick had told them? Was it true? Mike rubbed at the back of his neck, stopping when he saw Tina looking as if she'd gone into shock. Any more secrets and surprises, she might go mad. How did you comfort an angel? He sure as hell wasn't worthy of the job. Were any of them worthy?

"You can all relax." She tried to smile. "I'm feeling better. Having Rick come clean gives me a sense of balance now. At least we know where we stand. I have a feeling that because of ourstruggles to help others,we are the exception. The gods won't hurt us or let any harm befall us. We are probably what the gods are counting on to make the world a better place."

"So you do believe what Rick is saying?" Jack spoke up.

Trenchfoot cut in. "Should we doubt him? Is anything he's told us...up front and honestly...has it been a lie? As bat shit crazy as any of the things we know of in our world, why should this be any different?"

That's what Mike was afraid of. This was all really happening. It was bigger than any one of them, and Rick had put them together to work for a common cause.

"So what do we do? Where do we start?"

Tina came out of her reverie and said the most logical thing. "We start right here. With us...before we can help others we must help ourselves to find our peace." She stood up from the couch and took hold of Trenchfoot's arm. "Come on, Gold...let's go check on Tim," she turned around pointedly, "and let Mike and Johnny catch up on old times."

Damn. One shouldn't argue with an angel...immortal or otherwise. No telling what kind of shit she'd deal him.

"She's not only beautiful and sassy, but smart, too," Jack spoke up, clearing his throat. He nodded after her retreating form. "You two...um..."

"None of your fucking business." Mike turned on his old friend. "This is between you and me. Leave her out of it."

"I brought her here..."

"Yeah, you did. Why?" Mike folded his arms defiantly.

"Rick told me he was sending an angel to take care of the men we'd found. I didn't think she was mortal or a female. Delvante knew what kind of conditions she would be in. Why would he send someone like Tina? I was caught off guard but knew, from just the power I sensed around her, that Rick knew what he was doing."

"She's helpless, man. Naïve and too delicate."

"Somehow I doubt she's that naïve, if you two have been together—"

Really? Jack was going to piss him off. "If I hear any derogatory remarks about her out of your mouth, I will fucking punch your fangs down your throat!"

Jack backed off, his hands raised in surrender. "Chill man, it's cool. What happened to you? We used to joke around all the time about the trim we got."

"You happened—that's what. The war happened, life after death happened, you name it. If you are expecting me to be—"

"You thought you killed me?"

Mike stopped as Jack threw the vocal punch that had eatenat him for decades. He watched as his friend turned around and casually went to sit on the sofa, like a lion toying with his prey.

Mike closed his eyes, calming himself down internally. For years he'd wondered about Johnny, if he'd made the right decision to let the kid go into the compound, if something could've been different. He'd wondered what words he would've said to his friend if given the chance in Heaven or Hell.

"I'm sorry, Johnny. I should've never sent you in there. I should've taken my team in first—"

"Why? So you could be the 'all American hero.' You were always better than me, protecting me, keeping me from finding my own way." Jack sneered. "You weren't any different than my folks, always thinking I couldn't make it on my own. That I'd always have to rely on them and their money to amount to anything."

He stood up and walked up to Mike, pointing his finger in his chest. "I didn't need to rely on you. I was ready to prove myself come Hell or high water. I could lead a team as well or better than you could." Jack swallowed hard. "You never gave me the opportunity.

"I wanted to prove—" he paused to gather himself, "I wanted to prove to you I could do it. That you could rely on me out there, in the field, that wherever we went, you could rely on me, man." He turned away momentarily. "You were like the brother I never had. You'd always been there for me. You'd been bailing my ass out of hot water since the academy, and I was ready to prove to you I could hold up my end of a deal.

"Well, I screwed the pooch, didn't I?" Jack turned back around, wiping at his face and trying for a laugh that sounded strangled. "I sent each and every one of my five men straight to Hell. We never had a chance. Shit, the Charley's and the prisoners we were sent to rescue—they were already dead. We were just more food for the fodder. Some hero I am."

Mike sat quietly for a moment. Jack was right—he'd never given the kid credit or the chance to prove himself.

"I was still the team leader. The choice was mine to be made who went in first. I put you and the rest of your squad at risk. The fault lies with me."

"And what if I just belayed your orders and went in anyway. My men were first night watch. I could've had them go in before you gave us the go ahead."

"Would you have risked a court martial, John?"

"Damn right I would. And I would do it all again in a heartbeat if I had to."

"Knowing the outcome?" Mike asked solemnly.

Jack nodded. "Especially knowing the outcome. You're here, man."

For the first time since that horrible night, Mike felt a piece of burden lift from his chest, just a piece of the heavy shrapnel fragments he carried in his heart, but it was a good feeling.

Mike smiled emotionally. “No Johnny...we’re here.”

CHAPTER ELEVEN

Tina sat beside Timothy's bedside watching him empty another bag of hemoglobin that Trenchfoot had sacrificed for the turning. Mike had said the worst was over, which was true for the young man. There were vivid blue veins running like waterways on a map over his pale body. Anemia was one of the first symptoms they suffered, leaving them weak and pasty looking.

He was resting comfortably, peacefully. Even when she looked inside of him there was no torment or struggle within him. It was almost as if he accepted his new life. How many others were so willing?

An angel. She smiled.

Well, you were right, Marilyn.

So many times in her past, Marilyn had called her an angel for putting up with the bullshit from suitors who looked to her for comfort and then dumped her. Or the times that Tina let things go when Marilyn insisted she fight back. She was always too nice, or an angel according to her friend.

She wondered if Marilyn actually knew the truth. No, she would have outright told her if she'd known. Neither one held back secrets from each other—others, yes, but never from each other. No matter how hard it was to accept.

Tim stirred and his eyes opened. At first the swirl of mercury set his eyes to dance, but they settled and so did he.

"Are...are you...are you an angel?"

"Funny you should ask..."

"Whoa? Seriously?" He tried to sit up. "Am I in Heaven?"

"No. Germany." She put a hand to his chest. "You're fine, lie back and relax. You've been through quite a bit lately."

"There was a guy...or I thought...and..." He gave up and lay back wearily. "I must be having some pretty wicked dreams."

Tina didn't know what to tell him yet, if anything. She tried for a different bedside manner. "So, where are you from?"

"Nebraska."

"Nebraska?"

"Yeah, not much there so I thought I'd join the Army. I qualified for medic, and they sent me to train in action, right out of Boot Camp. Nothing like on the job field training."

"I bet." Tina smiled and tried to find something else to talk about. "You miss your family?"

"Don't have one. Well, I did, but my mom died when I was thirteen and my dad, well he was an alcoholic. We didn't get along. I ran away and ended up in foster carewith various families until I turned sixteen."

"What did you do then?"

"I found an abandoned moving trailer in the backlot of a salvage yard I worked for, went to school during the day and had a place to sleep at night."

"Didn't the owner worry about you?"

"Nah...he never knew. I would pretend to go home for the night but there was this hole in the back fence line not far from the trailer. It was clean, and I managed with a few odds and ends I found while I was working."

"Resourceful. I'm impressed." Tina sat back against the chair and crossed her arms. "So what ever happened to your father?"

"Beats the hell out of me. Don't know, don't care." He looked up at the nearly empty bag of blood. "What's with the transfusion?"

"You lost a lot of blood. We're making sure you're well fed."

"Damnedest thing about blood. I think I dreamed I was drinking it."

"You don't say?"

Mike, Trenchfoot—somebody. They needed to get in here and explain things before the kid found out on his own and decided to make a meal out of her.

* * *

"This is something Tina has to do," Jack said.

"I've heard enough about the legends and myths of the Dacians to know if the gods say it must be done, you don't argue with them," Trenchfoot added. "Look what happened to Rick and Aiden all those years ago. Pissing off the gods? Yeah, not my cup of tea."

Mike didn't want to listen anymore. Tina wasn't made for this. She was mortal and the god's, Rick and everyone else knew it. He'd been shocked to learn she was training for a position as a Shield. It took a strong, street-smart soul to be able to handle the job as an immortal's assistant. They dealt with danger on a constant basis and had to be one step ahead of their immortal and two steps ahead of the rest of the mortal world. But to know she'd become...or was an Angel?

"She's not going on the mission. She's not capable of handling the rogues," Mike argued.

"You didn't see her take on my vamps back in Dallas. I was hesitant about Rick's decision to send her on this job, but once I saw her in action..."

"Jack, I said no and I mean no. She's staying here."

"Whoa!" Tina came back from tending to their patient, walking in on their discussion. "I happen to be capable of making my own decisions, Mike. You don't have any say in what I do."

"It's too dangerous. We know what we are up against."

His beautiful imp stood toe to toe with him, her eyes flashing. What he wouldn't give to taste all of that bottled fury unleashed as they made love. She thought she could have the upper hand with him by looking so damn hot? She had another think coming.

"So I'll learn. I'm sure you didn't just come from the womb fighting rogue vampires."

"I'm immortal—unless they cut my head off or stake me out in direct sunlight to fry—I'm pretty safe. I never allow them to do either."

"Jack saw what I can do. He can vouch for my abilities at kicking some Vamier ass." She nodded in his direction, her hands planted firmly on her hips, daring him to tell her no.

"Jack's vampires are domesticated. We are dealing with

ones that have no off switch. They feed and bleed on instinct. They don't follow rules or guidelines from anyone."

"That's why I've been assigned to help them make their decisions. They weren't given the chance set forth by the dictates of the Dacian gods. They were turned without a choice. I can help them make that choice."

"And what if they don't want to listen to the golden haired angel?" Mike replied. "You gonna just let them drain your mortal blood?"

"Mike...hell man, give her a chance," Jack said. "She's an adult—and women these days make their own decisions."

"Not when they are part of my team. I make the command decisions." He snarled, not at Jack but directly at Tina.

"As always, Mike. As always." Jack sighed and sat down.

"Jack. Now is not the time..." Tina interjected, trying to keep the peace between them.

Mike turned on her. "Don't patronize me, Tina. You have no idea. This isn't about then, it's about the here and now. What we are up against. This isn't a group of guerilla fighters in the jungles of Vietnam, we are dealing with the creatures who do not die and will tear your throat apart for a taste of relief from a hunger worse than death."

She wasn't listening. She heard what he said but she wasn't really listening. The blank stare and tight lipped facial expression gave him that much information. Tina spoke up.

"Trench, how many more soldiers are there in the hospital wing at the Army hospital, besides Timothy?"

"We have about ten we've kept in various states of comatose until they could be seen to properly," Trenchfoot replied.

"How soon will I be able to get back there and see to them?"

"We can leave at dusk. But now it's time to rest."

Mike couldn't believe he was being ignored, defied and overruled by a snip of a woman. Was this what he got for scorning her?

* * *

Exhausted. Tina wasn't sure when she'd gotten her second wind in the past seventy-two hours. It wasn't her first time staying up for days on end—exam weeks were a good trial for the long hours but not the emotions that came with it.

Trenchfoot had given her a guest room that fit her perfectly. There were no doors just short corridors leading to chambers off of the main cave that gave enough privacy with their winding curves. Dark, quiet and restful. He'd turned on a small bedside lamp that illuminated the dark rocky shadows of the wall. She was literally going to sleep in a chamber of a cave. A small stream of water naturally cascaded over part of the rocky wall into a basin like a fountain in a spa.

After thanking her host and saying goodnight/good morning, she removed her utility belt, combat boots and the camo shirt. The cool air on her bare shoulders relieved some of the stress.

"What the hell do you think you are doing?"

Tina gasped at the sudden intrusion and turned. "Get out, Mike."

"Not until we talk."

"You mean not until 'you talk.' I have nothing to say. I'm tired. I haven't slept in over seventy-two hours, and all I want to do is crawl into that bed and die."

"Oh trust me, you're heading for the 'die' part easily enough. You are not getting involved with this mission. I don't give a damn what Rick or anyone else has told you—"

"Go away, Mike."

She cut him off and turned to pick up her shirt off of the bed where she'd tossed it.Tina turned back, folding it neatly. Looking up at him, she saw Mike's silver eyes dance with dangerous intent. He was pissed. Good, it served him right.

"I can't." The sheer rock walls seemed to absorb the sound of his words. But she heard them.

"Why? Did Rick order you to watch over me?"

"No." He let out a slow sigh. "I can't get you out of my head, Tina."

"Really? That didn't seem like an issue for you a couple of months ago." She nodded her head in the direction of the doorway. "Go find your 'other woman' to tell your sad tale to. I've moved on, Mike. Just like you wanted me to."

There was no emotion on his face, which kind of frightened her.

"There was no other woman, Tina. I tried to find the one thing that would make you move on. I only pretended."

"Well congratulations, you deserve an award for your performance because it worked." She unbuttoned the top buttons of her uniform pants and stopped as she saw his eyes travel there, hungrily. "So unless you are wanting to go over mission details with me for later tonight, I suggest leaving. I'm going to bed...to sleep."

He shook his head slowly. "This isn't over, Tina. You are not going out on this mission."

She dropped her trousers, stepped out of them wearing nothing but bikini cut cotton panties and a tank top. She folded them up and placed them at the end of the large bed with the shirt she'd removed earlier. The heat radiating from Mike intensified. His wild, musky scent filled her senses. She turned away from him so he couldn't see the hardening of her nipples, the need in her eyes.

Stay strong, Tina. Don't fall. You've come so far.

"I'm not yours to command, Mike. Take it up with Rick." She slipped under the covers and turned off the light, leaving him in the dark.

"Trust me, I will."

The final tone in his voice and the sound of his boots echoing away had her gathering the last bit of her restraint. She prayed to God to let her sleep one night without thoughts of Mike Linder haunting her dreams.

CHAPTER TWELVE

Tina woke up with a start.

"Shh...it's okay, Angel. It's just me, Trenchfoot," the deep gravelly voice whispered in her ear.

Rubbing the sleep out of her eyes and getting her bearings, she realized where she was. "What's wrong? Did I sleep too long?"

"No. It's early in fact. I thought you might like to head out to Landstuhl before Mike awoke."

Did she ever. Throwing back the covers she got out of bed and went for her pants. Trenchfoot turned around discreetly and cleared his throat nervously.

Blushing she realized what she had done. Nothing like showing off her delicates to a complete stranger. "I'm sorry, Trenchfoot. I guess I am just excited..."

"I understand, Miss Tina. But I'm still old school when it comes to ladies. Back in my day, a gentleman didn't view a woman in her underthings unless they were married."

"Unless a woman was a bit loose?" Tina teased.

"Don't ever let me hear you referred to in the same light as a 'loose woman,' Missy. If any man thinks otherwise, I will deal with him right away."

She buckled her belt around her waist, reached for her top and walked around the bed. "That's why you are 'Gold.'" Kissing the man's raspy cheek, she smiled as she put on her camo top and grabbed her gear.

"Don't let that get around," he grumbled as he led her out into the quiet hallway.

* * *

They made it out and on the road as the sun was setting behind them on another day. Tina relaxed knowing that she was free of Mike and Jack for now and could breathe a bit. Trenchfoot regaled her with stories of the War to End All Wars and the love of his life, Jessica. He'd kept tabs on her until the day she died back in 1986 at ninety-two years old.

She'd married and had a family. But he'd been at her funeral, secretly watching from the comfort of a tinted car. The only thing that made it easier was seeing that she'd had a rich full life of happiness, and she was surrounded by many who had loved her on her final day.

Would that be her and Mike? Would he watch her move on in life as he stayed forever young? Would she be happy? Even now she didn't think it was possible. Not without him.

Has he made you happy? Has anyone ever made you happy?

She could answer that honestly...but didn't want to dwell on the truth.

"Would you ever marry?" she asked out loud.

When Trench didn't answer right away, just kept looking at the Autobahn as it stretched before them, Tina wasn't sure if she had actually spoken the words.

“What you’re asking is not an easy question to answer. There aren’t a lot of mortals who know about us and immortals, well not a lot of women-folk.”

“But if you did meet a mortal and fell in love with her. What would you do?”

“I’m single for a reason. I can’t share my way of living with someone who wouldn’t understand. I couldn’t watch them grow old and become feeble while I stayed whole and never changed.

Trenchfoot looked older and wiser than any immortal she ever met. His salt and pepper hair matched a mustache that curved down around his lips. He had a long narrow face with hard angular lines that spoke of hard work and outdoors and ruggedness. There wasn’t anything “pretty” about Trenchfoot. He was what her father would refer to as a “man’s man.”

“How old are you?”

Laughter rumbled from his chest, deep and real. It put her at ease.

“Hell Angel, sometimes I feel as old as dirt...I’m older than some of it but younger than the stones that dirt came from.” He winked at her. “Don’t let the gray fool you, darlin’. I was gray before the War. I’d already aged fast, especially working the silver mines out in Arizona.”

“Really? You were a miner?”

“Yep. Got fed up with it though. All the killin’ and watching your back as someone tried to kill you for an ounce.” They were coming up on Landstuhl. He was watching the roads carefully. “I hooked up with the Calvary as they were heading in to monitor the borders. Joined up and the rest as they say is history.”

"You must've been pretty young." Tina looked away as they turned up onto the road leading to the hospital. "Come on. I know you were in the Great War, but how old were you when you were turned?"

"Older than most of the young men in my outfit." He sighed. "I was thirty-five, a captain in the U.S. Army, in charge of twelve men. We were under attack, but not by the Germans. I had just gone off duty to catch a few winks when all hell broke loose. A band of rogues came in and desecrated my squad. I'd been bitten but woke up enough to see my attacker. I reached for my knife that I kept on me at all times and sliced the creature's throat as it was still leaning over me. I was lucky enough to have been doused with his blood, managed to swallow a good portion. It's the only reason I'm here now."

They made it through the gate, even though technically it was closed for the night. The guard didn't look any different than a regular military solider standing gate duty, that was until she saw his eyes. The silver swirl...there was no doubt he was a Vamier.

"One of my men. Good guy." Trenchfoot nodded as he drove on up towards the hospital.

They parked in one of the back lots. The same one they had parked in the night before. It seemed like weeks had passed since then, but she knew they hadn't.

Trenchfoot turned off the ignition and sat there. He turned to her, narrowing his steely gaze in her direction. "You sure you're ready to handle this again, Angel?"

She nodded. "I'm needed in there."

"Yes you are. And let me tell you, there is no greater feeling than being needed."

That was the story of her life.

* * *

Eight patients were in need of her. Six were recently wounded and partially turned, only two, besides Tim, were victims more than a year ago.

Tina hadn't realized how draining it was on her mentally and physically to perform the "last rights" to the patients. Out of the first six, two decided to live with immortality and were being prepped for their transitions as vampires while she went about helping the last two of the comatose victims.

Her seventh patient was almost too far gone for either venture. His physical shell was riddled with injuries so severe that he'd never make a whole vampire. Internally his wounds were too damaging. Vital organs wouldn't be able to sustain the nourishment of a transfusion. Even in semi-death, Tina had to literally carry him to the door on his way to eternal peace. Never had she been more grateful to have a deceased family member on the other side take him into his arms. She'd wept with the joy of knowing he'd be taken care of by those who knew and loved him.

A young woman awaited her in the next room. All the rest so far had been males. This time, it felt more personal.

Laying her hands on the dark haired woman, she wasn't prepared for what she encountered.

Sitting alone like the others had, in the dark, she looked up and smiled. There was no surprise or shock.

"I know who you are."

"Excuse me?" Tina was taken aback to the point she looked around behind her to see if the woman was somehow talking to someone else. But as always, it was only the two of them.

"Did he send you?" The woman stood. Dressed in full Army fatigues, her brunette hair pulled back into a tight bun, she stood a good half a foot taller than Tina so possibly five foot nine or ten inches.

Tina had some rank recognition, the woman wore the insignia of a major. It was her first officer patient.

"I'm here to help you move on—"

"I can't move on. I have work to do." The major stood at rest, her hands clasped in front of her.

Tilting her head, Tina was not sure what to think. She should be the one explaining things. But she had no explanation.

"You do realize you are in between life and death?"

"Yes." She nodded. "I've known I would end up in this situation for a few years. I was told to wait for you. You are what they call the Immortal's Angel? Right?"

Confusion stalled Tina from making any more advances just yet. "I don't think I understand."

"You are here to help me decide if I want to go to Heaven or stay on as an immortal being."

Tina nodded. "More or less."

"I was bitten but not to be turned. I was bitten so you could bring me back.I'm not the immortal one, but I have to live. My daughter needs me home. She's the one who's immortal."

* * *

It was clear that Trenchfoot was as confused as she was. Tina's exhaustion and mental state right now did nothing to help her figure things out.

Major Pamela Griffith rode with them back to the fortress. The others who wanted immortality were being prepped to be flown privately to Livedel facilities back home in Maryland to continue getting the best treatment available during their turning. But Pam had no intentions of joining them.

"I told you I'm not immortal." She almost laughed at the brooding Trenchfoot who didn't know what to do with her.

"Then what the hell are you?" he thundered. "You shouldn't be here." Trenchfoot turned to Tina. "She shouldn't be here." He repeated as if she hadn't heard him.

"What am I supposed to do? I wasn't informed I'd encounter someone with her abilities." Tina defended herself. If this was another "Rick joke" he needed some educating on humor.

"Who sent you?" Trenchfoot interrogated her as he drove.

"I don't know. When my daughter was undergoing medical treatments as an infant, I had to take her to a special clinic in Maryland. I met with the doctor of the clinic briefly, and he told me my daughter had a special gift, a pre-ordained destiny. Ever since that day, I've looked for answers. Occasionally I will get letters from the clinic, keeping track of my daughter and my whereabouts and necessities.

"My most recent letter told me to meet a messenger from

the head of the clinic while I was on duty in Dubai. The letter stated I was to eventually meet with an Immortal's Angel and have her bring me back home. I would leave the military as missing in action and bring my child with me to Maryland. I went to the meeting place and was attacked. That's the last thing I remember."

"You said your daughter is 'immortal'? How do you know?" Tina asked.

"The doctors told me. But not in the way you think. She's not a shifter...at least I don't think so at this point," Pamela offered.

"What about your husband? Her father?"

"Not married. Never knew him." She sighed. "Look, I had a dalliance with a guy I met while I was on leave about eight years ago. It was a one-night stand—he was gone before I woke up the next morning."

"He didn't leave a name or phone number?" Tina asked.

Pam snorted and eyed Tina lazily. "Really? I take it you never had a 'casual' fling. You don't exchange name and numbers... just orgasms, Angel." She turned back to look out the front window. "I'm not the marrying kind of girl. I hate to have anyone in control over me."

"You were in the Army. I'm sure there were many who controlled you," Trenchfoot said.

"I'm here for one reason and one reason only...I was sent to get to this point in my life. My last message told me I would be meeting the man who will teach my child her position in life. So can someone tell me who in the hell is Rick Delvante?"

CHAPTER THIRTEEN

Pissed and pacing, Mike wasn't amused to find Tina gone when he woke. Not only Tina, but Trenchfoot, too. He knew where they'd gone but had no way of getting there. The only vehicle he knew of was the one Trenchfoot had.

Ranting at Rick for two hours did nothing to alleviate his frustration. With some of the words he used and names he called Rick, it would surprise him if he didn't hunt him down and have him put down as a rogue. Why the man hadn't yet was beyond his understanding. Each time Rick threw another fucking riddle or piece of assignment that was more bizarre than the last, Mike swore this would be the end of his eternal life. The pain in the ass could test his metal and vice versa.

"Would you calm down? What has happened to you over the years, Mike?" Jack had settled in as if there wasn't a care in the world.

As always, he'd had a nonchalant attitude about everything going on around him. Same old Johnny. Nothing fazedhim.

"I didn't see a ring on her finger."

"What the hell are you talking about?" Mike finally stopped pacing.

"Tina. I don't see a ring on her finger, so why are you pissed off at her not being here?"

"I forbade her to get into this...she doesn't understand the manipulative way Rick can be. She can't handle living among immortals. She's going to get hurt."

"Don't you think that is her decision to make? As I said, I don't see a ring on her finger." Jack shrugged. "So what happened between the two of you?" He leaned back, relaxing on the sofa. "She beat you in a game of chess? Out shoot you on the firing range? What?"

"Tina is not like that," Mike replied gruffly. "She's not like anything I've known." His voice quieted as he ran his hand over his face, feeling the never ending scruff he'd officially "died" with.

"Then why haven't you married her?"

"Really? You have to ask." Mike glared at his old friend.

"It's not like she doesn't know you're a vampire. Hell, she'd make a great addition to an old SEAL commander." Jack stood up. "Man, you have no idea. When I saw her in action...damn she had half of my best immortal troops down for the count. And when she nearly crushed one of Trenchfoot's men's spine from his head...she meant business. For a mortal, you could do worse, Mike."

"That's just it. She's a mortal. She's young, vibrant, alive... she needs a real life. Tina's a bookkeeper, not an assassin. She's not meant to take out demons and immortal beings that could kill her in less than a heartbeat."

"So you'd rather have her married to some staid, four-eyed nerd who can give her two children, a suburban home in a nice little cul-de-sac and no excitement?" Jack snorted. "What are you going to do? Watch from afar like some peeping Tom as she lives her life, grows old and dies?"

"I don't see you married with kids," Mike retaliated.

“Never saw myself with them. Not when I was mortal or immortal.” Jack grinned. “I like my occasional fling but nothing serious. I happen to like ‘fast food’ that doesn’t stay around too long and cramp my lifestyle. If you get my drift.”

The echo of footfall coming from within the caverns, followed by voices, brought both men on alert. Trenchfoot entered looking haggard and worn, rubbing the back of his neck. Tina and another female, taller, decked out in an Army major’s fatigues stepped into view, their conversation dying.

“Sonofa—” the dark haired woman looked straight at Jack. “It’s you.”

Jack stood up looking from her to Mike, perplexed. “I don’t think I’ve had the pleasure, Major.”

Leaning on her hip she turned to Tina and nodded at him. “Oh, yes he has...eight years ago.”

Tina’s eyes widened and she walked away, holding back from laughing out loud.

Jack still didn’t catch on. This woman knew him...intimately.

Mike cleared his throat. “Um, Jack buddy, I think your ‘fast food’ is about to ‘cramp your style,’ if you get my drift.”

* * *

The brunette walked right up to Jack. She was almost equal height, looking him in the eye. “Eight years ago in Austin, Texas.”

“I’ve been to Austin many times,” Jack retaliated.

“No. I guess you wouldn’t remember.”

"You seem to remember me, though." He smiled the charming, Johnny smile.

She eyed him up and down casually."Sure do...not because you were memorable, though."

Damn. The woman cut to the quick. Mike fought hard to hold back a grin. He looked over at Tina leaning casually against the wall. Fatigue darkened the porcelain skin under her eyes, yet she tried to smile through it all. Jack was right. He could do worse. But she could do so much better.

Tina stepped forward. "Jack, this is Major Pamela Griffith. Pam, let me introduce you to Jack Tabor..."

"Of Tabor Financials?" Pamela asked Tina.

"Matter of fact, yes," Jack responded.

"I should shoot you now." She shook her head with disgust. "Twenty-five years ago you closed down my father's auto parts store and three other businesses in our town."

"That would have been my father," Jack said in a form of apology. "I took over not quite ten years ago."

"Makes no difference to me. Tabor Financials still leaves a bad taste in my mouth."

Mike sighed. "Okay. Introductions aren't going so well here." He butted in. "Major Griffith, I'm Mike Linder." He held out his hand in greeting.

Pamela had a nice firm grip. It said a lot about a person, but he wasn't sure what to think of the Amazon woman, yet.

"What's the purpose of you being here?"

Tina stepped forward. “I brought her back to life. She knows about Rick so we thought we should bring her back here.”

“Whoa.” Mike assessed both women. Pamela didn’t look like she was on the verge of turning. She wouldn’t be standing if that were the case. “I don’t understand? Is she—?” He raised an eyebrow at Tina.

“Immortal? No.” Tina shook her head. “But her daughter is.”

Mike had no time to digest or respond. Trenchfoot walked back into the room.

“Foxtrot, the old man is on the horn. He needs a word with you.”

Shock and disbelief warred with the fact that Rick was calling to talk to him. He’d just gotten off the phone with him not too long ago.Things were going bat shit crazy and why, oh why did he feel like Rick Delvante had something to do with this?

* * *

“Linder here, Rick. What’s up?” Mike waited as the pixelated screen of the video chat came into focus.

“I hear you have a Major Griffith with you all, asking about me.”

“Well, not sure she’s asking about you. But she sure knows Jack.” Mike sat back casually at Trenchfoot’s desk. This was going to be good. “How does she know you and vice-versa?”

Rick swiped at his face, looking as haggard as an old man. That couldn’t bode well.

"Things are starting to come together quicker than I expected. I thought maybe a few years, a couple of decades at least... damn." Rick shook his head and blew out an exasperated breath.

"What's going on, Rick? Spill it. No more riddles or secrets. The more we know the more we will be able to prepare for. It's that simple."

"I know. I'm beginning to feel that way. I don't have a choice, not at this rate."

Mike leaned forward now, knowing that Rick had to come clean...at least for the most part. He was lucky enough to have knowledge of immortality and the alternate reality that made up the Dacian clans. Nothing could be more far-fetched if you knew those two certainties.

"I've been keeping an eye on Pamela Griffith and her daughter for a half a dozen years or so. It wasn't until a few years ago when we had Little Lucy in for testing that we were able to match her paternal DNA. When I researched the bloodline it led me to Jack. I kept close tabs on him, working jointly with our program when I found out he was immortal."

"I don't understand." Mike shook his head.

"I sent a medical team to diagnose her daughter when she started showing unusual signs of paranormal oddities. I had them take blood samples and DNA testing. Pamela is a Dacian blood carrier—"

"Like Marilyn's mother, Diane?"

Marilyn was conceived by an infertile, immortal Dacian only because her mother Diane had been a direct descendant of the true Dacian bloodline—before the family curse had gone into effect. Diane had been the only reason Rick had been able to link and produce a child.

"Yes."

"And Jack is definitely the father?"

"Yep. But here is something else I bet you didn't know—your friend Jack, is also a true Dacian DNA link."

Mike let out a breath. Yeah, this was getting a bit much. Two naturally born off-spring, one from a Delvante clan and one from a Vamier, all in less than a half a century. When nearly two millenniums had gone by producing none.

"How many more could there be out there?" Mike asked.

"I'm pretty certain a few more, so don't be surprised if we come across any more in our system."

"Why? What is going on in the clans?"

The pregnant pause meant that Rick knew more than he was sharing right now. He waited for Rick to continue. "Just tell me."

Rick nodded in agreement. But the pale, stricken look on the old immortal's face didn't bode well. Whatever he was needing to tell him was difficult.

"A new generation of guardians is emerging. The gods had foretold of this time but never indicated when it would happen, just that it would."

"Okay? Is this a good or bad thing?" Mike wasn't sure what Rick was trying to say. He knew Marilyn and Draylon were the new Guardians of the Dacian clan, but was he saying there was more than one?

“I’m not sure. We’ve only known our old ways and those we’ve adapted to. There has been a new breed of Dacian blood that have different powers, personalities and potential than what the elders are familiar with. There has been no word given to us by the gods as to what this means.”

“Wait, you’re saying you don’t have a clue what is going on with the new incoming breeds of immortals?”

“That’s exactly what I am saying. I can no longer guide and instruct on what I don’t know. All I know is that they are coming.” Rick paused. “I’m trusting very few with this knowledge, Mike. Please, don’t let it get out.”

“Who else knows besides me?”

“Draylon and Marilyn...”

“And?”

“Pamela Griffith. Her daughter, Lucy is a preordained Guardian.”

CHAPTER FOURTEEN

Having settled Pamela into a room nearby and checking on Timothy, who was recovering quite nicely, Tina didn't know what to do. She was tired mentally but physically she had the urge to go running.

Thanks, Rebecca. Am I addicted to running now?

Something told her Mike wouldn't allow her to go out at one o'clock in the morning for a jog in the woods. She'd been surprised to note he hadn't laid into her the moment they stepped into the room with Pam. But then there had been little time for Mike to confront her about leaving with Trenchfoot.

Still mortal, there was always the option of running during the day. Maybe with some proper sleep now, she could run while the vampire men were all sleeping. She'd even talk to Pam and see if she wanted to join her.

But that was hours away. She needed something to unwind her physical self now if she was going to get any sleep.

The den was unoccupied. Mike was probably still talking with Rick. Trenchfoot had a labyrinth of cavernous rooms to keep himself entertained in and Jack, God only knew where he could be. It didn't matter. She would sit on the sofa and listen to the constant drip of the water off of the stalactites until it lulled her to sleep...or made her get up and pee.

Soothing sounds of the water and the muted colored lights reflecting off of the natural walls and into the water mesmerized and calmed. Meditation had been her most difficult class during her training. Tina couldn't remember how many times she would either fall asleep or not be able to get into a deep enough trance and become frustrated. Well, they didn't have the natural surroundings they were in now. It was a perfect place to meditate.

"Hello?"

Tina snapped into alert status at the sound of a greeting. Mike stood over her with a bottle of wine and two goblets in his hands. His brow creased in concern.

"Are you all right?"

"Yes. Of course. Why do you ask?" She angled herself away from him a bit as he sat down close to her.

"I've been calling your name for the past five minutes and you haven't responded."

"Oh, sorry."

Had she zoned out? She didn't remember anything. Maybe she'd finally been able to get into the realm of nothingness her sensei had fervently worked to put her in.

Now she was awake and aware of her surroundings...very much so. Even with a cushion length between them, Tina was much too close to Mike for comfort. He poured two glasses of cabernet sauvignon for them and handed her one. It reminded her of the night she'd seduced him.

She wondered if he—

"Don't worry." He smiled. "I'm not going to drag you off to my lair like some barbarian."

Is that what he thought of that night? That he'd been a barbarian?

Taking the glass of wine he offered, she took a tentative sip and tried for a weak smile.

There were two things that could happen right now, he would start demanding to know why she'd defied him and left with Trenchfoot earlier or...she didn't want to think about the *or*. Tina wasn't sure she was ready for either.

"Relax. We are just sitting here drinking a glass of wine." He saluted her with his glass and took a healthy sip. The good thing was, vampires couldn't get drunk on just alcohol. The only way they could was if they were to ingest the blood of an inebriated victim. But that didn't stop her from becoming tipsy—and red wine was the one thing that did it to her. She could find herself in a precarious situation if she wasn't careful.

"Relaxing is not something I can do easily around you, Mike."

She calculated his every move as he sat forward and placed his goblet on the heavy marble coffee table in front of them. He sat back in the corner of the sofa, facing her, one leg propped across the other.

It was a sexy, sensual pose, leaving him physically wide open for her. Tina found herself hard pressed not to react. She took another sip of wine, trying to let it relax her like it should. Unfortunately he had her wired six ways to Sunday and damn if she'd lost track of what day it actually was.

"I know, Angel. I blame myself. I'm not an easy person to relax around. There was a time when things were different. A time not so long ago."

She placed her glass down on the table and jumped up from the couch. "Stop! You are trying to manipulate me. Don't screw with my emotions, Mike. You did that already."

"You want to talk about screwed emotions?" He followed her movements. "I've never met a woman who could infuriate me as much as you can and turn around and have me fascinated by everything you are. You're a beautiful puzzle I want to lay out and try to put together. And yet, I know once all the pieces are connected I would just destroy you."

"Why do you assume you will destroy me? What if I'm the one who destroys you? If you are talking about your nightmares and outbursts of violence—you've never seen me in action." She gestured wildly as she walked away. "I know what to expect, I am not naïve. Do you think Rick would have put me in this position if he thought I was?"

"Rick doesn't know what he's doing."

"Really? A man as ancient as he is and smart enough to have created a domain like Livedel and you don't think he knows what he's doing? He knows exactly what he is doing. I just don't think he knows how to go about handling it with others." She paused, leaning against one of the natural pillars. "Did you know my parents work for him and have for over sixty years?"

She knew Mike didn't know how to answer. He took a nervous sip from his goblet. He knew.

"They were there in Vietnam, weren't they? Did my parents help you turn?" Having seen her mother in action with the young officer before she left, and knowing everything Rick revealed to her, somehow she knew her parents had been there for Mike.

"Yes. I owe a lot to your folks." He confessed. "Mama Kaye helped me through the transition, sitting with me..."

"That's why they trusted you protecting me. They knew who and what you were."

Tina pushed away from the column. "Rick knew what he was doing all along...and so do I."

"Okay, I'm sorry. I'm skeptical of him, always have been... but then he's been there for me. It's a difficult relationship. I'm hell on difficult relationships it seems."

Tina steadied herself and walked back to the couch. Mike's arm draped over the back, his eyes closed as if in pain. She lightly stroked his muscular forearm, tracing the light dusting of hair.

"I had hoped that taking away some of the pain...seeing that Jack was alive...all of it, might release some of the negative past you've suffered." She spoke softly with emotion.

"You shouldn't have witnessed my pain. It's not for you to suffer." He looked up with adoration in his eyes.

"Maybe it is. I am after all the Immortal's Angle. Am I not supposed to help those who suffer move on?"

"You were trying to do that before you found out what you were. I'm not worthy of you succumbing to the terrors I deal with."

Tina walked around to the other side, her throat tightened with sadness for him as her body ached to be with him. She fought against the pull of wanting to touch, heal, be near him, but the magnetic energy connecting them wouldn't allow. As she straddled his lap, Mike adjusted for her to fit comfortably.

His eyes swirled with silver pools of the same desire she felt. The warm, musky scent of him filling her senses, the rigid protrusion snuggled against her and the heavy denim between them, spoke volumes. She laid her hand on his beating heart, feeling the erratic rhythm matching her own skewed pulse. Tina let the beat carry her, feeling the love he had to share, the fear of sharing it...

"Did you really get over me, Tina?" His husky voice cracked.

Her eyes closed as she felt the bleeding within his heart. She couldn't bear it anymore. Ruby tears fell from her eyes as she engulfed the ache.

Opening her eyes she saw the terror of how much the simple question meant. She'd never seen her immortal warrior so vulnerable.

Tina stroked his jaw tenderly with her finger. "Does this answer your question?"

Time stopped as she let herself touch her lips to his. Just a simple kiss, to feel his mouth against hers once more. With her hand still on his heart his soul let loose and wrapped itself around her as he did so physically. The kiss deepened, he tasted of wine and aching hunger. His hands clenched in her hair holding so tightly, embedding himself into her as his pain ebbed into pleasure. Pleasure she brought to him with her touch, her kisses, her body...her heart.

She was his Immortal Angel.

* * *

Mike stood with her wrapped around his waist. Tina didn't stop kissing him, absorbing deep pains within him as she deepened their kiss. Her soul hungered for the ache, drawing it out only to replace it with the physical pleasure they shared.

They were moving. She was being carried. One of his hands cupping her bottom while the other stroked her back. His taste, his heat intoxicated more than the glass of wine or any glass of wine. Mike was her drug and she would gladly succumb to overdosing on him.

The softness of her bed cradled her as his hardness dug into her. Mike's hands roamed over her, tenderly at first as if he were opening something delicate. Cool air met heated skin as she realized he'd opened the front of her shirt. He latched onto one of her breasts, his mouth surrounding the mound, his tongue drawing detailed designs around her nipple and areola.

He moved on to the other, tracing, laving, suckling as his fingers plucked the dampened twin he'd just tortured.

Tina fought to breathe. She was having trouble catching her breath as he loved on her.

Mike stopped, leaving her wet nipples to pucker in the chilly air. He grabbed her hips, lifting her ass off the bed to pull her pants off in one swift motion before planting himself in the V of her legs and lifting her to Heaven.

Her body throbbed and pulsed with every stroke of his tongue. Lifting her higher he brought her legs over his shoulders holding her at the perfect angle to eat his fill.

"Mi...Mi...Mike..." she gasped as his tongue circled her clit, lashing at it before catching it between his teeth. Tina squealed.

She ached to be filled with him...all of him.

As if reading her mind, he unbuttoned his pants. She felt his cock before she saw it. It lay heavy and swollen across her lower abdomen. Tina looked at it, the glossy head glistening in the soft up lights around her room. She looked up at Mike. His eyes swirled with their silver orbs, his jaw tight with control. He took himself in hand, guiding his long, thick shaft to her opening.

Tina had no time to prepare. Mike's hips lay flush against hers. He filled her completely. The satisfied groan echoing from his chest made Tina's muscles clench around him.

Throwing back his head, Mike worked his hips in and out. He would retreat until just the tip lay at her opening and then delve in with barely controlled thrusts. Wild and animalistic he impaled her over and over, each time a bit harder, a bit deeper.

"Angel...Tina...fu—" He clasped his fingers in hers, squeezing as he released into her.

She watched as his fangs emerged and he bit into his lip. Blood dripped onto her, and for some erotic reason, set her off. Bucking up to meet his final thrust she came, drowning in sensory overload as he pumped into her with every inch of him.

* * *

"You're up bright and early this morning," Pamela said cheerfully as she rounded the corner.

Tina didn't have the heart to tell her she hadn't really gone to bed. The small amount of sleep she'd gotten was peaceful and refreshing. That was why she was awake.

"I thought I'd go out for a run. I haven't in a few days so

need to do something to get rid of this pent up energy. You run?"

"Not as much as I used to but I need to get back into shape a bit." Pamela patted her non-existent stomach. "Lying around for a few months didn't do much for the physical part of me."

Tina wondered why that was. How had she been able to function so quickly from a comatose state? She hadn't been wounded...just bitten. Maybe she could get more answers out of her after their run.

Staying to the trails laid out in the woods near the fortress,they couldn't have picked a better place to run. The dense overhead canopy of pine boughs kept the warm June morning at a pleasant temperature. The dirt trails were smooth but contained obstacles of roots, rocks and pine needles at the edges of the terrain.

There wasn't another soul around. The trail emerged into lush green valleys, hillsides covered in vineyards and open fields full of thousands of solar panels. In the near distance, a row of tall, three blade wind turbines turned slowly. Trenchfoot told her of how Germany was one of the top countries in Green Energy. He enjoyed the ability to have his home powered naturally and to share that power with his neighboring villages.

"It's beautiful and peaceful around here," Pamela mentioned as they jogged together after taking in the scenic wonder.

"I know. I've never really had a chance to see it in the daylight. Jack flew us in during the middle of the night. I haven't been out during the day since I left for Dallas." Tina huffed lightly as she tried to stay in pace with the long-legged brunette. "By the way, what day is it?"

"How the heck should I know? I've been in twilight for a while. I thought you might tell me."

"Well, let's see...I arrived in Dallas on the night of the fifth of June. We flew ten hours across the Atlantic and part of Europe yet we didn't land until night fall, that would have been the sixth...I'm going to say today is the ninth or tenth but don't quote me on that."

Pam shrugged. "I guess it's all irrelevant anyway. Does time matter to most of the people you deal with?"

Tina stopped when they came to an overlook. Winded, she paced to keep her muscles from locking up. Pam backed up and jogged in place for a few moments until she too slowed to a warming pace.

"I haven't always worked with the immortals," Tina said.

"No? You just picked up the gift and started turning people?" Pam asked.

"No. I was trained."

"So there are more like you?"

"Not exactly."

"I don't understand." Pam shook her head with confusion.

Tina cocked her head. "Actually, neither do I."

They both laughed. Tina figured if you can't explain what you are or why you are, it was better to go with misperception.

* * *

Two intuitive women with nothing to do could only mean one thing...adventure. Tina had managed to locate a nearby town that was nestled at the base of the craggy hillside they were secluded away in. They searched the compound and found a group of bicycles up in a gardeners shed beyond the ruin's property. It wasn't like they were going to steal them and there was more than two there to choose from.

Well maintained, the bikes managed quite nicely in taking them down the steep, winding hills into the backside of the town. They passed residential homes painted in bright colors just feet off of the narrow one car streets.

The quaint village had a town square surrounded by lovely pubs and beirgartens ensconced behind small gates between alleys and restaurants. They found a patisserie/bakery with a café and stopped for a bite. A piece of Kruchen and a hot white chocolate was a perfect late morning treat.

"So tell me about yourself, Pam. What made you go into the Army?" Tina asked. She didn't know many military women at all, much less an officer.

"I had nothing better going for me. After my father's lucrative business went under—no thanks to Tabor Financials—there was very little money to be had for college tuition for me. My sister and older brother had managed to go, but by the time it came for me to go, there was nothing left.I did manage part of my associate's degree during my summer breaks my junior and senior year of high school, but that was on my waitressing tips."

"And you joined the Army after graduating from high school?"

"Active duty enlisted. I spent my first year mostly in Ft. Huachuca, Arizona for my job training, then a year in South Korea before being sent to Ft. Hood, Texas. While I was in Korea I was able to finish up my associates degree through an on-line college program offered through the Army. As long as I maintained a C or better it was basically free. So when I got to Hood, I continued with my bachelors and at the same time was sponsored by my commanding officer for the Gold Program and transferred to an officer's rank after making Sargent."

"So how did you meet Jack?"

Pam wiped the crumbs from her breast shelf and sat back, staring at her, but more through her. Tina wasn't sure if she would answer the question.

"A group of us had just graduated to officer. I'd also finished my bachelor's degree about the same time. We'd promised ourselves a weekend in Austin to celebrate." She smiled in remembrance and toyed with her used fork, smooshing leftover crumbs between the tines on the plate. "The group got a suite but I opted for my own King suite. I wanted to soak in a bubble bath and have room service all to myself.

"I went down to the bar after midnight. Not very many people were there, but I wanted a drink in the ambiance of the piano bar and soft lights. Don't ask me why. Maybe it was because I wanted to feel luxurious and see if I could find just a quick fix for the lack of sexual relationships I'd had since being at Ft. Hood."

"Maybe it was your destiny calling you." Tina quirked an eyebrow at Pam as she took another sip of the decadent hot white chocolate.

"It was something." Pam agreed. "I was sitting there, listening to the piano man playing *Smoke Gets in Your Eyes* and drinking my glass of scotch, minding my own business when he walked in."

Tina tried not to smile. The way she narrated was like those private eyes in the old movies, describing the "dame that had just walked into the joint."

"Damn. Talk about hot. This man had a grace and style about him that had nothing to do with the black tux he was wearing. The thick waves of his dark hair, the shadow of scruff...umm....I was tingling all over."

Yeah, Tina could see that about Jack. He did have a suave, debonair appearance that would put James Bond to shame.

"And when those eyes latch onto you and won't let go...a girl knows when she's done. My timer went off and that's all there was."

"So right there and then?"

"No. We eyed each other across the room. It was just the two of us by this time. But it was as if we had our own private language right away."

The deep wistfulness in her voice overpowered the rough woman Tina had interpreted her to be.

"The piano player started playing *Moon River* and he motioned for me to dance. There was no 'asking' or anything remotely polite. I don't think I even cared. The next thing I knew we were dancing. Me in a pair of black jeans and an off the shoulder summer sweater and him looking like sex on a stick in his tux.

"His gaze was so mesmerizing. I realized what it meant to

'drown' in someone's eyes. I don't know much more about how that part of the evening went. We ended up in my room and I... well, let's just say for the record, I haven't found anyone to compare in eight years."

"And your daughter?"

Pam sobered. "Lucy is the best thing that ever happened to me. My sister and brother-in-law have partial custody while I'm overseas. But I knew she was different when I had her. I could never believe a child could enchant those around her—without even speaking."

"What do you mean?" Tina didn't understand. Maybe it was a mother "thing."

"My daughter is mute. She's never spoken though she has all the physical ability to do so." Pam leaned across the table conspiratorially. "And yet she has a learning curve that has set her at a college level student."

"And this proves to you she's immortal?"

"No...but this does." Pam pulled out a picture of her dark-haired, angel faced daughter who looked to be about eight. On her inside wrist was a natural birthmark of a nearly closed circle, but at the end was the outline of a snake head with its mouth open, devouring its own tail, the Ouroboros.

Tina had read about the "symbol of eternity,""immortality" in her Ancient Dacian class as a Shield...this was the symbol of universal existentialism—the sign given only to those by the gods when a new phase of rebirth in the world took place.

CHAPTER FIFTEEN

Getting his bearings, Mike had to analyze where he was. This wasn't his usual room at Trenchfoot's. Raising his head off of the pillow he looked down his body to notice he was covered with a blanket, but underneath he was naked. Then he remembered and a grin flittered across his face.

He rolled over and inhaled the scent of spring flowers—Tina's fragrance. They'd stayed up talking, kissing and drinking wine and making love, too. The first time was wild and frantic. He had to have her. The next was slow and sensual with her riding him to Heaven. Drained, she'd fallen asleep curled around him, her hand resting on his chest along with their bodies coiled around each other like a protective blanket. It had been so comfortable, her head snuggled under his chin, inhaling her, wanting to drink her in and hold her essence in his heart forever, even if it might be his last chance.

He hadn't intended on falling asleep.

Stretching, he lingered, wrapping his arms around her pillow. He'd missed her. It took him forever to admit it, but damn if he didn't.

Looking at his watch he noticed it was later than when he usually awoke, which set his mind to race. He felt good. No, he felt great. When had he slept so well that he woke up so refreshed? He couldn't remember.

Usually there were inklings of leftover terror, heart palpitations or anxiety greeting him like the sun used to. Was it the wine? No, he'd had wine before bed many times, it never changed anything. He rubbed at his chest, feeling the warm lingering of where her hand had rested.

Mike stopped and contemplated the situation. Each time Tina had done that, laid her hand on his chest, over his heart, he noticed another weight of burden being lifted. Could she be the reason behind him feeling this fantastic? Nah, it had to be coincidental...and the fact she was in his messed up world again.

Stretching and shaking his limbs to get the blood flowing, he headed out into the main corridor down to the den to see who was up and about. Anything new happening, Trenchfoot would be reporting it. The guy had eyes and ears everywhere. Truthfully, now that the soldiers were taken care of from Landstuhl, he wondered what their next task would involve.

Walking into the den, Mike noticed Pamela and Trenchfoot sitting on large cushions around the marble coffee table playing chess. He looked around as he went to the refrigerator full of hemoglobin.

"Where's Jack and Tina?"

"They're out on a mission," Trenchfoot said casually, watching as Pam took his pawn.

Mike stopped. "What mission? You all have taken care of the Landstuhl patients."

"You think it stops there, Mike?" He shook his head. "No son, that's why I called in the heavy artillery. Jack and his team are pros at going in and flushing out the flock. He got word over the day that there've been some sightings over in Nuremburg."

"So why does he have Tina?" Had his voice raised in panic?

Was his heart beating with anxiety because she was gone?

"Tina works for him, now. Rick sent her on this mission with Jack...I can't tell you any more, Mike."

He needed to sit down. Panic raced around his body like a hyperactive child. Was Jack up to the task? Could he handle the mission?

"When did they leave?"

"Over an hour ago." Trenchfoot got up from the game. "Relax, Mike. Jack knows what he's doing. He's been training Vamiers for a couple of decades now."

"Tina's with him. Anything could happen."

"Or nothing could happen and they finish the mission and come home," Pam added.

"You don't know her..." Mike groused.

"And you do?"

Trenchfoot stepped in between them. "Okay. Let's not get into a pissing contest, pardon my French, Major." He nodded at Mike. "Go look in on our young Corporal. He's just about ready to be on his feet. He'll need some training. Since you finished his turning, you should be the one to take care of him."

Great. They were putting him in charge of the kid so he didn't lose his shit over what was going on with Tina and Jack. Hell of a diversion.

* * *

"Hey, I know you." Timothy McCain peered up from the tablet he was reading and greeted Mike. "Where's the hot chick?"

"Watch your mouth, kid," Mike growled.

"You two bangin' it out? Don't blame you in the least."

Mike let go, punching the kid in the jaw with so much force it knocked him out of the bed and onto the floor on the other side.

Tim slowly maneuvered up, holding onto the side of the bed with one hand and his lopsided jaw with the other. "I 'ink u 'oke 'y 'aw!"

"Your jaw will be fine in a few minutes. As long as your neck is still intact consider yourself a lucky sonofabitch. I hear anything like that out of your mouth again, and I will make sure you end up as a pile of ash."

Picking up the electronic tablet off the bed, he studied what the kid was reading. Trenchfoot had provided him with videos and files of documentation bringing Tim up to date with the present. He'd been in limbo for eight years, there was a lot to cover.

"You learning anything?"

Tim nursed his jaw as it began to heal. " 'eah. Don' 'iss off an elder."

"That's right. Don't piss off your elders, especially ones who are assigned to take you under wing. You never know what they might do. They could have you run errands for them during the day."

The kid looked confused.

"You can't be out in daylight without frying, Tim. Might as well get that through your head now before making the mistake later."

"What if I forget?" He wiggled his jaw with amazement at how rapidly it healed.

"You won't forget again, I'll tell you that right now. The first time is a bitch."

Mike sat down with Tim and went over any questions he might have about his new condition or anything on the tablet that might need an explanation. Learning there was a black commander in chief was a bit of a shock and that half the country had approved same sex marriages had him a bit confused. The market dropping, foreclosures, gas prices, and half of his favorite actors passing away was a downer. And who in the heck were the Kardashians and why were they so important to the world as he had to know it now?

"So now what?" Tim asked.

"Well, you'll have to spend about six months at Livedel in Maryland to learn the ins and outs of being immortal. They will access your needs, provide you with a job source within the domain and clan and set you up in a private location."

"Sounds cool but six months? Basic Training wasn't that long.And that was a pain in the ass," Tim groused.

"Six months is equivalent to a second in the life you will be living now. Take it for what it's worth."

"Will you be guiding me at Livedel?"

Did the kid sound wistful? Why would he want him when there would be so many others to connect with?

"I don't know. We'll see what happens." Mike got up from

the edge of the bed to leave.

"Hey, I don't even know what your name is or what I should call you." Tim stopped him.

"Mike. But you can call me...Mike."

That made the kid laugh. He wasn't used to making people laugh. It felt kind of nice.

"Mike, sorry about the incident earlier. What's her name? She's very pretty." Tim shied away. "I thought when I woke up the first time here she was an angel."

Nodding that the apology was accepted, Mike smiled. "Her name is Tina Johnston...and she is an angel."

* * *

It was well past two in the morning and still no word from Jack. Mike had been pacing since he knew they'd been gone, and now Trenchfoot was watching the clock as if he knew they should've called or reported in...even that they made it safe.

But he also knew the old man was keeping an eye on him, making sure he didn't go off the deep end. It was a stand-off of sorts, neither wanting to alarm the other and starting a war over command decisions.

Mike could feel it though. Something was wrong. His gut instincts told him something wasn't right.

"Has there been any radio contact that they even made it there?" Mike asked.

Trenchfoot shook his head slightly. "They were under radio silence."

"You do know that this does not bode well, Trench. We should've heard something, anything."

"I know, son." Trench sighed and looked over at Pam who'd fallen asleep on his couch. "I was going to give them another hour, just incase, but my patience is wearing mighty thin right now."

Mike nodded at the sleeping form. "Did you know about her? She has a daughter..."

"Yeah, I know. Rick informed me when I brought her in at Landstuhl. She needed a medical excuse to leave the military and take care of her daughter. Rick sent some of his team in to let her know she was needed at home."

Looking at the clock again Trenchfoot waved him off. "Go check the ComStat. See if there is any word."

Mike was familiar with the set up. He was the one who'd built and installed the massive commcenterso it wasn't an issue for him to utilize.

Nearly running through the corridors to the communications chamber, he didn't even sit in a chair. He went to all the satellite readings and checked on homing devices. Slipping the headset over his head he didn't see any. Malfunction?

Going through all the security checks and specifications rapidly, nothing seemed amiss. Where in the hell were they?

Trenchfoot came in behind him leaning over his shoulder, studying the radar screen. "Zoom out."

Mike zoomed out, but there wasn't a trace anywhere within the flight path or even into Austria and Switzerland.

"Who were the crew members with them?"

"Jack took a group of his trained men who he'd dispersed when they first landed in Germany earlier this week. He'd sent them out to scout the area and report back. According to their findings, they had a rogue group to put down and victims that needed Tina's guidance."

"Where in Nuremburg? Did they give a location?"

"They were using the old grandstand in Zeppelin Field."

"I'm heading out there..."

"Not without me."

Mike and Trenchfoot turned at the breathless tone behind them. Jack leaned in the doorway, bloody, covered in a layer of ash and looking like he was about to collapse.

Trenchfoot went to his side and told him to sit down.

Jack shook his head, "No time...I'm sorry, Mike."

"Where's Tina?" The anguished catch in Jack's ragged voice had his heart ready to explode from fear.

"We got there and found the stash of victims. There are at least fifty of them inside the old Nazi grandstand. I left one of my best men with her to provide aid and support." He paused for breath. "My men and I were scouting the surrounding area, making sure she was safe inside when another group of rogues came along.We were out numbered. They just kept coming."

"How many more?" Trenchfoot asked as he looked at Jack's various wounds.

"About thirty that I counted, but these guys are not your

typical species. I was bitten in a few places before I managed to smoke my attackers. We are going to need reinforcements if we plan to get back in there."

"These open wounds should've healed by now." Trenchfoot looked up at Mike.

Mike was wrapping his head around the fact Tina was still there. She was mortal and dealing with God only knew what, besides half-turned vampires. Angel or not, she was a mortal woman...his mortal woman.

"I'm going in. Trench, do you have any men to spare?"

Trenchfoot nodded. "I'll send you a squad of my best. We'll get Tina out of there, I promise."

"Wait! I said I was going, too." Jack tried to stand upright.

Mike shook his head. He didn't know what had happened to Jack. This was the first time in his immortal history he'd seen rogue Vamier bites that did not heal. Yeah, not sure what they were dealing with. "You look like my cat who'd been attacked by two Dobermans...you aren't going anywhere until those nasty wounds heal."

Going to the weapons closet across the room, Mike geared up with an arsenal. He took things he probably didn't need, but dealing with the unknown and protecting Tina...he'd demolish half of the city if he needed to. "What am I looking for when I get there?" he asked Jack as he slammed a razor star cartridge into a hand held launcher.

Most of the time rogue Vamiers were individuals they hunted down and took out. The occasional posses had a unique tag or some indicating factor to them.

Jack gave a short laugh. “You’ll know them when you see them—they’re wearing Nazi uniforms.”

CHAPTER SIXTEEN

The amount of victims were beginning to overwhelm her. Tina needed a system if she were to have more situations like this in the future. She'd been so busy she wasn't aware of the time or where Jack and the others had gone off to. He said he'd be back, that they were going to scout the area. The only other person with her was one of the men Jack had left to help and keep her protected. Heath was a godsend. He helped keep the bodies sorted, the ones who were empty shells needing proper burials from those needing medical treatment to finish the turning process.

Tina managed to fight back her horror of watching Heath do an initial feed. The way he bit into his wrist to give the ones turning immortal his blood kept her nausea just on the edge of her esophagus. She tried not to look, but she would then have to immediately feed them from the bags of hemoglobin Jack and the team had brought with them just for this occasion.

"Heath, you need to rest and resupply your own blood," she said as they finished prepping another one for immortality. "There's a few minutes while I attend to the other souls."

Nodding, Heath stumbled among the graffiti and urine infested hall of the old grandstand ruins to the deep alcove where they had stored their gear. He sat down heavily on one of the tarps they'd laid out. Tina knew he was weak and exhausted. Sharing his blood with nearly thirty infant vampires had to be taxing on even the hardiest of Vamiers.

Quieting her mind and soul, she once again went to help the

next victim. A young woman, she'd been out jogging the steps of the grandstand when she'd been attacked, and she had no desire to become immortal.

Tina nodded and helped her find the door to her own beautiful peaceful eternity. Making her way back, something stopped her. A brief moment of pain and darkness...but she was still alive in the darkness and couldn't find her way out.

"Someone help me! Heath? Jack?" she cried out into the surrounding blackness. There was light and with light came hope...until she realized the light came from her.

"God, help me..."

* * *

Mike couldn't get close enough to the site with his vehicle. The surrounding streets were crowded with emergency trucks and gear. Large hoses connected to fire hydrants snaked around under his feet.

Zeppelin Field was a quagmire of mud as the fire fighters fought the blazing concrete remains of a symbol of what was once a great and terrible empire. But that was not what shocked him. It was his heart dropping out of his chest. The ache was so great he literally bellowed at the top of his lungs. His knees gave out, weakened by the heavy burden bearing down on him, and he sank to the ground in agony, cursing and ranting to whatever gods had done this.

What seemed like an eternity later, the fire was under control and rescue crews were carrying out bodies in bags. He needed to investigate. He needed to see for himself if one of them was his sweet, sweet angel.

He spoke to the authorities, making them believe he was someone sent to identify the remains. Each bag they unzipped was just another face. Surely they were someone's loved one or family, but to him, they didn't seem important. Body after body came out from the carnage, he'd counted fifty, but not a single one was Tina.

With his charade still intact, he meandered into the wreckage. Not much was really damaged internally. The thick concrete walls had been designed as a sturdy structure for a reason. Mike was thankful for that in a way.

The dark smoke infested area didn't bother him. He stayed and investigated every inch of the long corridor in which the infamous Nazi leader, Adolf Hitler once walked. Mike could almost feel the evil lurking. There wasn't a trace of anything to give him any clue to Tina's health or whereabouts. The only saving grace was the fact none of the bodies removed were her.

If that is the case, where is she?

A small, dark alcove at the end of the hall caught his attention. Deep in the shadows he saw an empty bag of hemoglobin—Livedel Industries on the sticker. He picked it up and hid it in the inside pocket of his gear vest. It wouldn't bode well to have that get picked up by the actual authorities. Rick would have a shit-hemorrhage.

Upon further investigation he noticed boot prints in the layer of dirt, mashed plant life that had tried to grow between cracks in the old foundation. Using a combination of his tracking skills from his days in combat and his unnatural instincts as a vampire, he was able to deduce there was a scuffle and many others had ventured in at one point.

The tracks led further into the alcove where there was an old iron exterior door. He inhaled the odor of kerosene mixed with—flowers? Was his mind playing tricks on him? Not now, damn it! But he swore his senses picked up the faint but familiar fragrance that had haunted his dreams for the past two months...Tina. She still might be very much alive. That tiny bit of hope was all his weary heart and mind were going to hold on to.

* * *

Heading back out, he gave the "thumbs up, all clear" sign to the rest of the local investigation team as he casually made his way back to the darkened BMW he drove. The tinted windows were perfect for protection on the inside and out. No one needed to see the interior, which looked more like it belonged in a war zone than on the urban streets of a major city.

"Gold Miner this is Foxtrot, over." He called to Trenchfoot's local at home.

"Go ahead Foxtrot...what's your status?"

He relayed the information about the fire and the body count of the dead.

"The Angel wasn't among them. I repeat, the Angel was not among them." He sighed but his voice still shook.

There was a brief pause as there was conversation in the background. Jack must be there too.

"Foxtrot you said the body count was fifty, is that correct?"

"That's affirmative, Gold Miner. Fiver-Zeero."

"Body count should've been fifty-two if all were accounted

for. That would have included The Angel and her Ace." Trenchfoot paused, talking to Jack in the background. "Joker says he left an Ace in the Hole with the Angel."

There'd been someone else with her? Maybe he'd managed to get her to safety.

"Is there a tracer? I repeat, can he be traced?"

"Negative, Foxtrot. Wait, belay that last—"

Mike could hear another voice, female in the background—something about radar instrumentation on camouflage...

Bingo! Hell, why didn't he think of that? He'd developed much of the tracking system software for some of the new uniforms being made for the military. Not only could the pixilation on the material protect them from enemy radar, but certain top secret frequencies could also trace them.

"Foxtrot, the Major is equipped to handle the task. Part of the Major's MOS."

"Roger that." It was the first good news Mike had heard in a while. "Let's get on it, people!"

* * *

The wait was worse than the worrying. Mike had to find somewhere to go for the day but yet stay close enough in contact. He ended up getting an inner room at the nearby Hilton so he could revive himself. Had it been just last night that Tina had been in his arms?

Lying there tossing and turning, wondering about her ate at him. He wished he had the kind of connection Draylon had with his mate, Marilyn. In times of duress they were able to communicate telepathically. It was how Marilyn was able to rescue Dray from her Uncle Aiden's fortress in Romania.

Even if she were in dire circumstances he'd still be able to be there, talk to her and give her hope. Hell, who was he kidding, he needed to hear her voice to give *him* hope.

Maybe if he just lay quietly and thought about her...

An alarming knock sounded on his door. Mike jumped from the bed. No one knew he was here. Was it housekeeping? No. It couldn't be, he'd put a Do Not Disturb sign on the door. The rapid knock came again. This time a patterned staccato of knocks.

Dot dash dash dash, dot dash, dash dot dash dot, dash dot dash...silence and then it repeated itself.

Morse Code. He knew who it was. They used to practice codes and semaphores for fun at the academy. He raced to the door, looked out the peephole. Sure enough.

Mike threw open the door. "Get your ass in here, Jack."

"Uh...not until you put some pants on man. Put that away."

Mike looked down and noticed he was naked and went for his pants. "How'd you know where to find me?"

Jack walked in and went over to hold up Mike's camouflage top. "Love your security satellites. You have an investor for your enterprise?"

Mike buttoned the large buttons on the fly. "Yeah, Delvante. He beat you to me."

"Shit. We made a great team before, we could do so again."

"The only team work I want right now is finding Tina." He

raked his hand over his head to smooth his mussed hair. “What are you doing out in the middle of the day?”

Jack’s brow rose in question. “Look at your watch. It’s ten o’clock at night.”

“No way! I just lay down.” He had, hadn’t he?

“Well then you got more sleep than I did.”

“How’s your wounds?” Mike asked his friend, remembering the ordeal he’d gone through earlier.

Jack rolled up his bandaged arms where the wounds were. “They’re healing better since Major Pain-in-the-Ass took care of them.” He grunted in indignation. “But it’s a slow process for some unfathomable reason.”

Yeah. Mike had never seen anything like it. It was almost as if the bites might have contained an acid based venom? That was unheard of in the immortal world.

“But I’m not here to cry about the Major.” Jack rubbed the back of his neck. “She’s actually been a big help. Her MOS is Military Intelligence in Communications. She was able to track the digitized uniforms with only a bit of an issue.”

“What’s the issue?”

“My uniforms that I have on stock and supply my teams with are a bit older. The technology is newer so we had to modify some things so we aren’t a hundred percent accurate.”

“Just tell me, did you find her?” Mike sighed. He’d deal with the minute issues with scanning equipment later.

“We think we found her...but if it is her. We aren’t getting a heat signature from our source."

Mike didn't want to hear that. No heat signature meant their source had either removed their clothing or they were dead.

* * *

The signal of their only possible clue to Tina was a warehouse outside of Nuremburg. They were out on a limb though, literally. Jack had suggested climbing one of the sturdy trees nearest to the warehouse and tall enough to reach the roof. The warehouse had glass ceiling tiles which looked down over the open bays. Moving from the tree onto the tiled ledge around the outer perimeter of the windows, they stayed in the dark so their reflections wouldn't cause shadows on the concrete floor below.

Mike nodded to Jack silently. Looking through their high-powered binoculars, he noticed a squad of goose-stepping, khaki clad lads formed outside the warehouse main doors. A convertible sedan, straight out of a World War II movie, pulled up and three official looking officers in black SS uniforms stepped out as a fourth man stood in the car.

The three men saluted...

"Heil Gerlich!"

Rolling over onto his back, Mike tried like hell not to burst out laughing. Jack took a second look. Confused at Mike's reaction.

"Gerlich Vamier," Mike whispered. "Draylon and I had dealings with him a few months ago in Maryland."

Gerlich had become Aiden Vamier's right hand vampire after Aiden "disposed" of Trevor Lyon's ashy remains for failure to bring Marilyn to him when she was under Draylon's protection.

But he thought Marilyn had taken care of Gerlich when she stampeded Aiden's fortress looking for Draylon. Looked like he managed to escape the devastation of a pissed off, female Zmeu.

"Nazi? Really?"

"Former Nazi soldier who still holds the führerin high regard...now it seems like he is da fürhrer."

Jack made a motion indicating "crazy."

"Pretty much," Mike whispered back. "That's what I'm afraid of."

Watching silently as Gerlich inspected his troops, they waited until "the fürhrer" went inside. Was there going to be a rally?

It took a few moments, but Gerlich and his security detail stepped a few feet outside of visual range for Mike. "Can you get a bead on him?" he whispered across the panes of glass to Jack.

Jack nodded. "Unfortunately he's screaming something in German—but then it all sounds like yelling to me. He could be wishing them, 'happy hunting' for all I know."

"You never really passed your foreign language classes at the academy," Mike groused.

"If I would've known I'd be in this situation—I would've." He nodded his head. "What about you?"

Mike sighed. "Only enough to get by, greetings, asking directions to the head...Wait, I wonder if this can pick up any words or phrases?" Pulling his mobile phone out of his utility pocket, he flipped through his apps.

The voices, especially Gerlich's, were loud enough all of Deutschland could hear. But whether or not his phone would be able to pick it up and translate was an entirely different situation.

Jack followed with his phone. Between them, they might be able to gather the gist of the conversation.

"...and furthermore, we will once again be the strongest nation in the world! This time, there will be no defeat! We are immortal. The mortal population will bow to our greatness..."

Mike rolled his eyes. Gerlich's mom must be so proud. Still, this was important information to tell Rick but not their primary reason for being here.

"They're bringing someone in..." Jack stated, reading his translation.

Mike readjusted his position so he could see what was going on inside the warehouse.

Two armed Nazi's wrangled a camouflaged man between them. His arms were tied behind his back and his combat boot covered feet were shackled with leg irons.

Jack sighed. "Heath...one of my men. I'd left him with Tina."

This wasn't boding well.

Gerlich walked up to him casually and slapped him across the face with leather gloves.

"Verräter!"

Mike knew that word. "Traitor?"

Jack's brow wrinkled as he listened.

"You think you can take power from me by taking the Immortal's Angel as your own? Your mission was to capture her for me...she would've been a powerful ally."Gerlich paced back and forth in front of Heath, each time slapping him with his gloves.

"I am still loyal, my fürhrer. I will train her to do your bidding," Heath pleaded.

"No! She is soiled. You have made her unfit to be my Empress." Gerlich snapped his fingers to someone in the distance.

Another soldier came out carrying a limp body in his arms, still dressed in the camo they'd tracked. Mike adjusted the goggles to see the details and gasped. It was Tina. His angel. Jack placed a hand on his arm and shook his head. He knew Mike was about to crash through this ceiling and kill every vampire in there to save her.

Gerlich looked at Tina's prone form. He turned her head, revealing two puncture wounds in her neck. Mike's heart sank even further. She'd been bitten. She was in the very limbo she helped other victims from. Somewhere between death and immortality.

Had Heath bitten her?

"I can take her away. We won't be a problem I swear," Heath begged. "No one has to know."

Gerlich walked back over to Heath and grasped his chin in between his fingers. "Ahh, but you see—I know. I will not be able to sleep wondering if you might have revenge in your heart. And if I can no longer have her, no one else will either."

Mike's heart cringed in fear. He knew what Gerlich was going to do before he did it. With the sharp blade to Heath's throat, Gerlich watched Heath's immortal blood being drained into a pool around him...not reserving a drop for Tina's turning.

Heath's body crumbled into dust at Gerlich's black booted feet.

"Nooo!" Mike crashed through the ceiling panel without a thought or care.

CHAPTER SEVENTEEN

Rolling from his jump over thirty feet, Mike didn't hesitate to take out the first shocked Nazi wannabe. There was not a single thought in his head, and pure adrenaline and anger fed his motions.

Chaos erupted and six vampires came at him at once. Taking out his blade launcher with one hand and a deadly, jagged hunting knife with the other, he made short work of fileting heads and having them seared to ash within seconds. Ash piles told no tales.

One jumped him from behind, a knife held to his throat...a quick back thrust of his knife into the abs made even a vampire double over which made a perfect angle for a nice clean decapitation.

Mike had no idea where Jack was and didn't care at this point. His only concern was Tina. He had to get to Tina.

Piled boxes and crates wrapped in plastic made great obstacles and leverage to get the hit on those trying to pinpoint a perfect angle on him. He'd learned over the years how to "dance" his way around an enemy's aim. Taking out two more focused on narrowing their aim, it was almost too easy.

"Schnell! Schnell!" Gerlich ordered as his security team kept by his side, their weapons drawn.

Another group of six came out from nowhere. Mike shot at three, taking down two, but mysteriously two more went down as a rounded blade launched from somewhere to the far right of the building. Jack.

He'd always been a hell of a sharpshooter and a sneaky bastard. Mike didn't react, kept his eyes peeled on incoming activity and took down the last of the six.

Gerlich screamed something in German, and Mike turned to see him heave Tina up in front of him like a human barrier. His Luger pistol trained flush against her right temple.

"I will shoot her!" he bellowed.

Mike knew that if he did, there would be nothing left of her. She would be gone. At least in the state she was in, there was a fighting chance...maybe.

"Put down your weapons."

Damn it! He was at their mercy. Not only did Gerlich have his pistol trained on her, his goons had him in their sites. This was a no win situation.

Mike raised his hands and carefully lowered his weapons to the floor, keeping his eyes focused on Tina and the pistol at her head.

"Now, kick them over to me."

From the corner of his vision Mike saw movement among the crates. He registered the subtle nod from Jack hiding out of view.

"Schnell!" Gerlich hoisted Tina up as her form began to slip and cocked the Luger's hammer back.

Quickly Mike kicked his weapons over towards them. Gerlich motioned for his men to gather them and that was all it took. Everything happened so fast it played in slow motion in Mike's mind.

Jack leapt out from behind the boxes and managed to launch double blades to take out both SS vampires. He threw his knife with a quick aim at Gerlich. Mike's breath hitched as he watched the blade heading straight for Tina.

At the last minute, Mike swore Tina's body dropped on its own, but surely Gerlich just lost his grip. The timing was so perfect Gerlich's only response was shock as the knife plunged firmly into his abdomen.

Curiosity and relief replaced the shock as a look of realization came over his features, and the fürhrer began to laugh manically. "You didn't kill me," he said, pulling out the knife and tossing it to the side.

"We have no intention of killing you, Gerlich," Trenchfoot and a dozen or so of his men appeared from the back opening in the warehouse. "Your trial in Dacian Court will make the Nuremberg Trails your friends went through sixty years ago look like an episode of Judge Judy."

* * *

Pam had been kind enough to handle the care of Tina's body and put her in comfortable clothing for the trip back to Maryland. Mike had contacted Rick to let him know what had happened. Rick promised to let her parents know and have a private staff at the facilities waiting for her.

He made sure he touched base with Marilyn and Draylon. Marilyn informed him she would be on the next flight home. The wedding was less than a month away. She could get married anywhere as long as she had her best friend beside her.

Mike was just numb. Sitting on Jack's Lear jet surrounded by opulence, he was aware of nothing but the silky feel of Tina's hair running through his fingers. He didn't want to leave her side. She was technically still alive. Occasionally he thought she would move an involuntary flinch that could just be associated with the nervous system. Her heart still beat, weak and thready,but it was a good sign. He placed a kiss on her cool forehead.

Pam removed her seatbelt and slid from the soft leather reclining seat to crawl over to where they were on the sofa. She'd come along to meet Rick Delvante and get settled in her new life as a civilian among immortals before she retrieved her daughter. Jack stayed behind to follow up with getting Gerlich shipped safely to Dacia under tight security but would be returning to Dallas within the next few weeks.

"Hey." Pam reached for his hand. "You do know she's still alive, right?"

Mike nodded. There was no way to speak without showing his true emotion. Mike squeezed Pam's hand to show his thanks for her tenderness and support.

"You could complete her turning."

"No." Mike shook his head and tried clearing the huskiness from his throat. "Not unless I ask her and she agrees to it."

"So you're not going to risk the Dacian code of ethics for someone you love?"

"I love her enough not to put her through that kind of hell."

"What you are saying is you want her to die?"

"What I am saying is she deserves to live or die how she wants." Mike's voice raised with a bit of anger.

"Or be left in an eternal darkness..."

Why was she doing this to him? A few moments ago she was all sweet and supportive, and now she was about ready to have him tear into her.

Pam placed a kiss on Tina's forehead and settled back in her seat. A tiny smile of satisfaction pulled at her lips. She was definitely odd. Damn her, Jack deserved the Major and all of her quirks.

A full crew of medical staff met them at the private airstrip in the mountain range. Rick Delvante was there to oversee everything along with Kaye and Jon Johnston, Tina's parents. Kaye was an emotional mess as Jon comforted her. Mike felt horrible, like he'd let them down. They'd counted on him to protect her, and he wasn't there when she'd needed him the most.

Walking away, he knew she would be under the best medical care in the world. There was nothing more for him to do. It was just him. Finished with another assignment. He should return home and bury himself in his workload. But work, life, whatever he was used to didn't seem to matter anymore.

He watched the emergency mobile unit take Tina away. There was no way to reach her, and he realized he'd just lost another man to battle. There would be no getting over the loss, and he'd gladly suffer the horrific nightmares to remind him once again that he had failed his mission.

* * *

Bleary eyed and hung over, Mike maneuvered from his pillow to stare at the alarm clock by his bedside. But it wasn't making the horrible noise piercing his eardrums. He flipped his tablet over.

"Mike! I know you are in there. You don't want me to get mad. I haven't learned to control my damn tail yet."

Who the hell?

"Get off your ass! Draylon told me you would probably be smashed. Don't make me go all Zmeu on you!"

He peered at the tablet again showing the security camera view from the front of his house. Marilyn Reddlin-Delvante was beating down his door, ringing his doorbell like a crazed woman in a bad, campy horror movie looking for sanctuary.

"You have until I count to ten to open this door...and then god's help you. One..."

Shit!

Throwing back the covers he stood up and tried to find some pants. The only thing he could find were a pair of sweats lying on the floor. When had he worn them?

"...five..."

She was rambling on about some crap in between counting like a mother disciplining her child.

He couldn't find a shirt. Not that any of them would be clean anyway.

"...seven..."

"I'm coming, for Christ's sake!" he screamed at the top of

his lungs, knowing she couldn't hear him and regretting doing so as the sound ricocheted around in his very tired brain.

He dragged himself up to the upper level of his domicile and threw open the door.

"Hey Marilyn..." He tried to smile, be charming to his best bud's fiancée, but he felt like Hell.

"Mike...oh my God! You smell like you haven't taken a bath in days." She held her nose.

"What night is it and I can tell you if I had one recently."

"It's July twenty-seventh...

"You're shittin' me?"

He fought to calculate the days. He'd been back in Maryland for five.

She muscled her way past him, which wasn't too difficult in his current state and continued down into his domain.

"Really, Mike?" She looked around his den.

Empty bags of blood lay around in various areas from gorging on the stuff. Clothes were tossed willy-nilly.

"Hey, that's where that shirt went." He brought it to his nose and tossed it after getting a whiff of what consisted of old blood, body odor and booze. Mike tried to calculate how it had gotten all those scents.

"What the hell have you been doing?"

"Beats the heck out of me."

"You've been feeding on winos downtown after closing."

Marilyn grabbed his arm and pulled him down the hallway to his room."Jesus!" She gasped.

The odor of old dirty clothes, socks and whatever was under the piles of clothes *was* kind of pungent. He was kind of scared to find out himself.

Still being propelled by the mahogany haired immortal princess from his room to the bathroom, she managed to turn on the shower with one hand and tossed him bodily into it with his sweats on.

"Shit, Marilyn!" The water was ice cold.

She handed him a body brush. "Scrub...or I'll do it for you."

"Like hell you will—"

She came at him, threatening.

"Fine, fine!" He grabbed the brush from her before she did. "Aren't you going to leave so I can shower?"

"Nope, I'm sitting over here, out of your way. Go ahead, I've got my own man to worry about. So you don't have anything I haven't already seen."

"Draylon sent you, didn't he?" Mike scrubbed his chest and face with the soft bristled brush Tina would use when she showered here. "Damn it!" He tossed the brush out, and it landed where Marilyn sat on the toilet seat. "You did that on purpose."

"Yep." Marilyn replied.

He cursed and decided if he had to get himself together then he might as well take a real shower. He shucked off his sweats and threw them towards the door. "Don't come around here. I'm getting naked."

“Thanks for the warning. Do you have any clean clothes?”

“Hell if I know,” he replied before sticking his head under the cold spray. Readjusting the temperature he soaped down his body and tried to find some semblance to his screwed up brain.

He rinsed off and stepped out of the shower to see Marilyn standing in the doorway to his room holding a towel out like it was a dead rat.

“Holy sh—” Mike grabbed the towel from her fingers and wrapped it around his naked hips. “Give a man some modesty. I’m sure Dray would be a bit put out about you seeing his best man’s junk.”

“I’ve been living in Dacia the past few months. With all the shapeshifting of the wolf clan...seeing naked guys walking around is common. They all think they have something special I haven’t seen before. I’ve even laughed at the few who thought they were all that and a bag of fun. It deflates their pride a bit.”

“You are as cruel as you are beautiful. Dray is in for a helluva ride.”

She shrugged. “He hasn’t complained yet.” She returned to trying to find him some clean clothes to wear. “Here, these seem to be mostly clean.”

He put them on. “What brings you here?”

“Your salvation.”

* * *

“I guess we’re here because your dad is wanting to ream me a new one for not being available,” Mike said as they walked into the front doors of Livedel.

"My *father* is pissed, but he's got a lot on his mind other than your moods."

He followed her into the elevators and didn't even register where they were heading until they arrived at the basement three level.

"No. Oh no...you are not doing this to me, Marilyn. I don't care if you are my best friend's mate."

"Yes. And I am," she stated once she stepped out of the elevator.

While still inside, Mike reached to push the door closed.

"You push that button and my father will have your ass! You don't want me destroying Livedel because you've angered a Zmeu."

"I don't care what you do. I am not going to visit Tina."

"That's because he's a kitty." Another woman, one he'd never seen before strode up to add fuel to the fire.

"What?" Both he and Marilyn turned to her and asked.

"A kitty—a derogative word for a weak man."

Marilyn cocked her eyebrow at the beautiful blonde with glitter powdering her cheeks and eyelids.

"Sariana, that would be 'pussy.'"

Sariana. Where had he heard that name before? Maybe it was a common name among women now. Mike could have pushed any elevator button and gotten the hell away, but something other than Marilyn's foot in the door stopped him.

"Pussy...kitty...same thing." Sariana eyed him. "This is what

Christina is all hot and bothered over?"

"Hey! I'm right here. I can hear you." Mike sighed.

"No...you are not 'right here.'" Sariana stepped into the elevator with him. Her five foot nothing, elfish frame stood toe to toe with him. "You are 'right here.'" And she slapped the side of his head like an Italian mother disciplining her young son for taking the Lord's name in vain.

"You talk about helping others, but all you've ever done is worry about 'you'—'oh poor me, I survived when others perished,' 'oh, the love of my life is gone, I killed her, I could've stopped them, I should've been there—'" the tiny pain in his ass over dramatized. "Cow poop! All of it!"

"That's bullshit...not cow poop," Marilyn corrected.

Sariana turned on her and waved a well-manicured finger in his friend's mate's face. "You're next, demon. Don't get it in your head just because I am thousands of years old that I can't kick your ass. I am still a Dacian goddess."

Ah hell! That was where Mike had heard the name. She was the actual woman who had started the divide among the Dacian clans. She'd brought the curse down upon them. She was the Zmei bride who Aiden had fallen in love with and went to capture, causing the destruction of all the Zmei except Draylon and the unborn Zmei bloodline she carried.

"You will do your deed Mike Linder because if you don't, you can add the destruction of the Dacian world to your inventory of failures and possibly the world as the mortals know it, too."

"And just what is my deed?"

“The hardest one you’ve ever undertaken.” Sariana looked deep into his eyes.

Mike could see thousands of years play like a video as he stood mesmerized. Her hands raised to his temples and his skull filled with heat, pressure...not uncomfortable, just weird and worrisome. His head lolled back weakly on his spinal column like it was too heavy for his neck to hold up.

Sariana released his temples and suddenly the pressure and heat dissipated, leaving an empty feeling of all coherent thought.

“You will stop thinking about yourself, Michael Linder. It’s time to use your heart and head to help those in need of what you alone can give them. You were pre-ordained to be here by the gods. Now is the moment to take your rightful place among the Guardians of Dacia.”

CHAPTER EIGHTEEN

The room was dark and quiet. He should've been in heaven, no light to cascade down on him and burn him to a crisp, no disruptions of chaos and chatter to make his brain explode. Yeah, dark and quiet was his interpretation of heaven...but not when the one person he wanted to share his ideal heaven with was unconscious in her own hell.

There were no wires or instruments attached to her. Tina just lay there in the dark, pale and beautiful...yet just this side of life. He didn't know what to do. Sariana had him step into the room and the door locked behind him. At first he'd been pissed, being manipulated by the goddess and Marilyn—God help Draylon if he was going to be saddled with the Zmei pain-in-the-ass mate. Maybe when this was all said and done, he could convince his buddy not to marry her. She was a witch with a capital "B."

Time had stopped. Mike had no idea if days or only hours had passed. Time usually stopped for most people when they stepped onto the Livedel compound, but this was even more of a finality of the universal time continuum shutting down.

An inner door opened and Kaye Johnston strolled in. She walked right over and placed her hand on her daughter's head and one hand on her heart. But it was brief and nothing changed. Two bags of hemoglobin were placed on the side table.

"How is she?" Mike managed to croak out.

"I don't know—I'm not the Immortal's Angel. Just her mother."

“But I’ve heard of Mother and Daughter bonds. There is nothing stronger,” Mike stated.

“By whose standards?” Kaye tilted a brow at him.

“Come on, Kaye. I know you, I’ve seen the magic you and Jon do when you two work together. You bring life back to the dead...” He sat forward in the chair where he was sitting vigil over Tina, clinging to hope that Kaye could save her, that somehow she possessed the same traits as her daughter.

“Immortality Mike.” Kaye shook her head sadly. “Not life.” She turned around to leave.

“Why torture me by bringing me here? Do you know how painful it is to sit next to someone you love and know she is neither alive nor dead? That she is in a state of limbo worse than hell? And there is not a damn thing you can do about it?”

The emotion in his voice caught, making his words harsh and angry.

Kaye turned around. “So you love her?”

Mike had tried for months to deny what he knew he felt. He did it for her...no, he did it for himself. The realization of thinking he was keeping her safe from him, from his kind of lifestyle, from the pain he suffered on a regular basis, it wasn’t for her protection, it was for his.

“Yes. I love her,” he admitted freely.

Kaye scoffed and waved as she walked away. “Don’t tell me. Tell Tina.”

The heavy door closed and once again he was alone.

You're not alone, Mike. Tina is right here. As you sleep during the day, you are as if in death but you are still there.

Could it be that simple? Was she spiritually still here inside her shell of a body?

Kaye seemed to think so, and the woman hadn't steered him wrong since she had helped with his turning. She'd been there, administering the drugs to help the pain, holding him like a child during the tremors, but most importantly talking to him—telling him that he was going to be all right, that she'd be there for him if he ever needed her...he remembered hearing those words and even then, not once had he thought it meant anything.

He sat forward in the chair and leaned over the edge of Tina's bedside. She lay there like Sleeping Beauty, pale and beautiful, her blood red lips bowed, her head resting in the nest of golden curls.

"Hey," he said quietly. He cleared his throat and tried again. "Hey Angel, I'm here. Umm...it's me, Mike. So...yeah..."

How did one talk to an angel?

"Man, I'm screwing this all up. You're probably laughing at me, aren't you, Tina. I know you. But I deserve it, I'm such a shit." He laughed.

"I don't deserve you. You are not only beautiful on the outside, but you have such a beautiful heart and mind. Any man would be so damn proud to have you for his wife...I tried to push you away to give you the opportunity for a full, rich, happy life with someone who could give you a family...

"Did you know the thought of someone else's baby inside of you just makes me want to punch a wall every time I think about it? I'm selfish, though I try to be practical. Hell, am I even making any sense? I'm babbling. I'm not a touchy-feely kind of guy... if I can't shoot it, stab it or kill it in some way, I'm not a man. Maybe that was just my generation..."

Mike talked, just talked about anything and everything, his feelings, what was going on, what Marilyn had done to him, meeting Sariana and even going so far as to let her know how much her parents had done for him, how much he owed them. He wasn't surprised that she was their child...love only begets love.

* * *

Tina sat like the others she'd helped had. So this was what it was like...constant darkness in an empty nothingness. Well, it wasn't exactly dark, not with her illuminating aura. But still, it was lonely and boring. There was nothing but quiet. Once in a while she would hear voices, but they were far away as if just mumbles in another room.

Didn't anyone know she was here? Was she too far gone? Why hadn't someone at least finished turning her? That was what they did before she came along. But she was still here. She'd even tried to find the doorway to the other side, thinking with her light it wouldn't be difficult. But there was no door. She couldn't find the way like she had with the others. Maybe it wasn't a natural instinct when you were doing it for yourself.

"Hey." She heard a voice like it was hovering over her. "Hey Angel, I'm here. Umm...it's me, Mike. So...yeah..."

"Mike!" she screamed. He'd found her. "I'm here. Can you hear me?"

She stopped and heard his voice talking about her being beautiful, about how her folks had been so wonderful when he went through his turning. How he'd taken for granted everything his immortal world gave him when all he'd ever wanted was to make amends for his past.

"Did you know I haven't had any nightmares about Nam since the night you and I were together at Trenchfoot's? I woke up so refreshed. It was like this heavy weight had been lifted from me. Maybe it was knowing Jack was still alive...I don't know. But I know it was because of you that I feel I have a chance at really living again, even immortally."

Tina smiled, tears filling her eyes. The sound of his voice comforted her but knowing he was opening his heart to her... God, she was the richest woman alive. Well if she was still technically alive.

"I love you, Mike." She could feel the tears fall.

"Hello? Can anyone hear me? She's crying...the Angel is cryingruby tears!"

"Come on! I know you can hear me, you all are monitoring us...Tina is crying. That has to mean something."

Tina continued crying. Tears of happiness because Mike sounded so elated.

"Now she's crying rainbow tears. What the hell does that mean? Come on! Rick, Kaye...Sariana, anyone!"

"Hey baby...come on. I know you're there. Come back to me. Wake up."

Another voice or two joined in nearby. Bright light nearly

blinded her and she screamed. *"She's there all right. Just waiting to be brought back."*

"Well bring her back, Jon. This is your daughter."

"It's not my ability to bring her back, no matter how much I would love to."

"Then get Rick to do it or Sariana...someone with some higher authority," Mike badgered.

"They can't do it either."

Tina felt the gentle peace of weight on her heart and forehead. Somehow she knew they were her father's hands.

"There are no other Immortal Angels. They would be the only one to help her make that passage."

"Are you sure there are no other Immortal Angels, Mike?"

"That's what I was told."

"Well, it's time to learn the truth."

"You are beginning to sound like Rick...riddles and unanswered truths. Give it to me straight, Jon. What is the truth? Is there another Immortal's Angel?"

"Yes there is."

"Who?"

"Her mate."

Tina listened intently to the muffled conversation between Mike and her dad. Her mate? She didn't have a "mate" that she knew of. No one she'd ever dated could fit the description of an Immortal's Angel. And how was she supposed to find one in the comatose state she was in?

* * *

Her mate? Like hell. Mike tried hard not to think of Tina having a "mate"—someone who could bring her back to life. But if there was someone who could do it, would he be willing to let her go?

Yes. He loved her enough to want her alive again. And if she had to rely on her mate, someone capable of giving her that chance, he would step aside and let him do what needed to be done.

But how would he find him? He was stuck in this room without any ability to communicate or research. No phone, no laptop, no internet...nothing. He wasn't even sure there were electrical outlets.

He talked to Tina, tried to reason with her to give him some clue as to men in her life that may be her true mate. But of course, she didn't answer.

The longer he sat and tried to figure out what he needed to do, the more frustrated Mike became. When he was about ready to tear a hole in the underground room to tunnel out in search of hope, the door opened and in stepped Kaye to do her morning rounds.

"Kaye, I need your help. Jon told me the only way for her to live is to find her mate, the other Immortal's Angel. Can you possibly tell me who might be her mate? Someone she'd dated in the past or knew through school or something...anything."

Rolling her eyes,Kaye seemed to sigh in what sounded like exasperation. She shook her head. Placing her hands on Tina's heart and forehead briefly, she looked up at him and smiled.

"You're as bad as everyone else. Smiles, rolling of the eyes, not answering questions straight forward...damn you, damn you all!" Mike stood up and threw the chair he'd been sitting on across the room.

He'd failed so many and yet the pain of the past diminished under the aching thought of losing Tina, not having her to hold, to argue with, to make love to...Mike leaned against the wall and thumped his head rhythmically against it, trying to find some way to staunch the flow of emotions aching within his chest.

Clenching his fists he only wanted to smash them into something, someone—but he couldn't and the defeat of feeling so hopeless ate into his heart. Sagging a bit he shielded his eyes from Kaye. She didn't need to see him break down like this. His vision blurred. Though his chest ached with a need to burst forth screaming...something, he couldn't. There was nothing vocal to go with the tears.

The pain was worse than turning, worse than the sun feasting on his skin. The emotion took over his body, twisting and tearing into him. His eyes filled with hot moisture, and he somehow knew he was crying. But the sound of pebbles hitting the concrete floor had him looking around.

Down at his feet, Mike saw tiny black obsidian gems scattered as another gem fell from...his face.

It didn't hit him right away. Stunned disbelief had him shaking his head as he stared across the room to where Kaye stood beside her daughter's bed.

Kaye's subtle smile and cocked eyebrow turned into a full-blown smile and a nod of her head.

"I'm...I'm...no." He shook his head and bent down to retrieve one of the stones. "It's black...why black?"

"What are your emotions that brought you to them?" Kaye asked.

"Anger, frustration...hopelessness."

"Black moods...black gems." She shrugged.

"Am I?...Is she?..." Mike couldn't say the words, his emotions were such a tangled web of confusion.

"Only one way to know for sure." She motioned for him to come closer. "Bring her back. It's up to you."

"What am I supposed to do? I haven't been trained."

"Give me your hands."

Reluctantly he held up his hands for her.

Kaye placed them exactly where her's and Jon's had been—one over Tina's heart and the other on her forehead. "It's the entrance to the soul. Now, focus only on Tina. Release everything else in your mind."

Mike looked down at Tina. "What if she doesn't want to come back? What if she chooses eternal life instead?"

"Then you must let her go."

* * *

Tina had heard. This was her option for an immortal life or life everlasting. Her choice would be permanent whichever she chose. But she wouldn't take an immortal life unless the one person she wanted would be willing to share it with her. She would base her decision on what he did or said.

A soft glowing light illuminated the far reaches of the darkness surrounding her. Mike stepped forward and she stood up. She tried to smile but with the look on his face she wasn't sure.

"You are a pain in the ass. You were supposed to return with Jack but noooo, you had to stay to help turn the victims. Did it matter in the long run?"

"Well hello to you, too. How have you been? Me...alone in the dark."

"...alone and pissed."

"That seems to be your natural state. So what's so different now?"

Mike sighed. "I still can't choose your path. I have to let you decide. I'm not good at that. I'll admit it, I'm a selfish bastard. I've been so wrapped up in my own distress so long that maybe I don't want to be saved. It's safer to feel sorry for myself and take the blame for the past than to go forward into uncertainty...into something I have no control over."

"You want to control me, control situations that aren't yours to rule over..."

"Yes. I'm a control freak. There I said it. Are you happy?"

"Matter of fact I am. Acknowledgement of the issue is the first step in recovery."

Mike laughed. "You're so damn cute when you're smug."

"So you have a control issue. Anything else?"

"Yes...I have post-traumatic stress disorder. I need help to get over the past. Since the night at Trenchfoot's when you witnessed my past pain, I haven't had the nightmares, but I know there is so much more I need to go through in order to put the past behind me."

Tina couldn't help but smile even though inside her heart was beating erratically at knowing she'd taken a layer of pain away from his internal wounds. But now that the scab had been pulled off, it was good to hear him say he knew he needed help. He was willing to try to find a way to let go.

"And..." Mike began.

"And?" Tina cocked her head.

"I have this horrible addiction that I can't seem to shake. I wake up at the end of every day hoping to see sunshine beaming down on me. For so long it had been cold and dark in my world, and now I dream of sunlight and warmth seeping into my skin, my bones...my soul, my heart."

"You're immortal. You know you can't be out in the sun."

"You think I'm talking about our large star this world revolves around?" He reached out to touch her face, stroking his thumb along her lips as he cupped her cheek. "I'm talking about the angel whose aura guides me, frustrates me because all I want to do is lie in her light and be wrapped in the warmth of everything she is. And yet, what does she do? She warms everyone's heart, beams her light for all of the unfortunate misguided souls to follow—

"I'm selfish Angel. I want you all to myself and yet I know I can't have you...no, I shouldn't have you. But I can't fight the addiction, and I'll be damned if I even want to try. So there. I'm broken, wounded, a control freak, a vampire with PTSD—a walking nightmare who is so damn in love with you..."

Tina felt the liquid tears flow. She cupped Mike's hand closer to her cheek and turned her face to nuzzle it, loving the rough callused feel against her skin, his thumb wiping her tear.

She cleared her throat. "Umm...part of your job is to give your patient the option to choose immortality or eternal life. You haven't done that yet."

"Do I have to?"

Tina nodded. She knew it was a mandatory endeavor as the Immortal's Angel.

"Christina Johnston, you have the option to choose an eternity with God and those loved ones who've gone before. Or, I can lead you to immortality with a grouchy, stubborn, control freak who loves you more than he knows how to express...but he will try every damn day, night, decade and century we are together to prove to you how much he does. I don't know what I can promise otherwise, there are changes going on in our world..."

Placing her finger on his lips, Tina shook her head. "Nothing is set in stone. Nothing ever will be. But I can't think of going through a life of immortality without you there to be a pain in the ass, constantly harassing me, arguing with me, just as long as you are loving me." She looked him deep in the eyes. "Can you promise me that? If you can't, I'd rather die."

"I think I can handle every one of your conditions."

"Good. Then lead me home, Mike."

EPILOGUE

"We're going to be late." Tina giggled as the best man tried pulling her back into the bed.

"Only 'fashionably' late. Besides, you don't think the bride and groom are doing the very same thing?" Mike stretched his neck to look at the clock on the bedside table. It wasn't really ticking the minutes away into the future...just giving them a sense of reference to agendas.

Besides, this was Dacia. The True Romanian's version of Paradise—an oasis where time was forgotten and immortality reigned supreme, nestled in a mysterious realm inside of the Hoia Forest.

"We have time for one more round." Mike waggled his eyebrows and threw back the covers exposing himself. "If you want."

"Give me a minute. I'm thirsty." Tina had set the coffee pot to their wake up time before the wedding. She went to pour herself a cup of the strong, black brew.

Mike's eyes narrowed on her naked form as she sipped from her mug. He lay there, his hands pillowed behind his head, beautifully erect and sculpted, like a fine piece of artwork to be touched and examined up close. Walking to his side she trailed her fingertips lightly over his abs. She loved watching them shiver and flinch. Letting them drift downward they followed the 'V' of his lower abs that pointed directly at the nest of wirier curls that supported his rock hard, exquisite piece of male anatomy...

and it was all hers.

"Is it time?" he asked.

She took another sip of coffee, eyeing him over the cup. She nodded slightly.

Mike sighed. "You are a control freak, my love."

"You agreed. I could have control here..."

"I know." With very little reluctance, he handed her silk curtain tie backs. Holding out his wrists to her she tied the curtain ties around them both, making sure they were secure before forcing them up overhead to be tied tightly above him to the brass headboard.

Once he was tied, she sat down with her coffee across the room from him. Sipping slowly, seductively as he watched, she teased the rim of her cup with her tongue and dipped her finger in the brew to rub around her nipples. The heat of the coffee enhanced her already sensitive buds and she moaned, arching her back from the chair.

Tina trailed more coffee coated fingers from her breasts down to her aching pussy. She could feel the excitement forcing her fangs to elongate. Biting into her lip, she let the streams of blood run over her torso and pool in the small indention of her navel.

Mike watched. Excited swirls of his silver orbs added to the sexual tension between them. She could smell his scent. The musky aroma of male animal in heat only made her want to break this terrible tension. Control was a two-edge sword—a bitch. But she needed to do this, she needed to assert her dominance over her mate and prove she could give as good as she got.

His shaft lay thick and heavy, the main vein standing out in deep purple relief across his lower abs, twitching like a fish on dry land, seeking the life giving ocean to breathe again. Standing up with her coffee, she walked back over to him, admiring the man and his gifts.

She removed her hand from the side of the warm mug she held and cupped his heavy sack between his slightly parted thighs, gently rolling the delicate orbs inside between her fingers. She wasn't sure if it was a purr or a growl that Mike emitted.

Looking up at him, she saw his eyes lidded in lust, and she sat down beside him, taking her time, caressing and massaging with light pressure, watching him react to every manipulation. His cock twitched, a bead of preliminary cum decorated the top. She wiped her finger across the tip and sucked her finger clean. The tension and heat in Mike excited her. Her nipples puckered into hardened stones, juices began to flow heavily from her center as she thought how hot he was and that it was because of her.

His head lolled in agony from side to side, his arms straining on his bindings, making the headboard shake. She smiled up at him, coyly, her fingertip clenched between her teeth. Taking another sip of the warm coffee, she held it in her mouth, letting the brew transfer its energy to her. She swallowed and immediately engulfed his cock with her hot mouth.

Pulling and sipping simultaneously with her lips, her fangs scraped lightly against the fullness of him. His body bucked and heaved like a tortured man. Managing to get his feet under him on the bed, he arched upwards.

It was a perfect moment for her to grab hold of both of his

ass cheeks.Their hard, musclesclenched while he breathed out heavy groans. The deep roll of her name from his mouth threatened her with a good time with each dip of her head.

Mike was shaking, his whole body in a cataclysmic tremor. The sound of metal ripping from its moorings, the whoosh of air as a piece of headboard and silk cords flew across the room didn't stop Tina from having her chance to give him pleasure. That was, until she felt her body being pulled from him and flipped over onto her knees.

She gasped. In one firm, dominating motion, Mike buried himself pelvic deep into her from behind. His calloused fingers dug into her hips, forcing himself deeper and deeper with each thrust into her womb. Now it was her turn to lose her mind as he lifted her up, pressing her into his chest as he drove up into her harder and harder.

His musky scent and sweet sweat lathered her body. His hands cupped her breasts, squeezing at them roughly, his thumb and finger pinching her nipples until her body was strung so tight she was going to explode. His hot breath whispered in her ear as he nipped her earlobe and thrust up and forward so quick and hard he hit her "g-spot" and sent her soaring into oblivion.

Mike bit down into the tightly corded tendon of her neck and shoulder, feasting on her sexually heated blood. The aphrodisiac was a satisfying joining of two mates, marking them as their own. How many times had they each done it to the other since the turning? Tina would never be able to keep count. But her scent and mark were on him as his were on her.

His body stiffened. Every muscle in him tense and strung taught. He came with a roar of release both vocal and physical, setting off aftershocks in her body until both of them were drained.

They collapsed on the bed, exhausted but at peace.

* * *

"Where have you been? I was worried I'd have to get married without my best friend up there with me," Marilyn asked as Tina hustled into the room where she was to change and prep the bride.

"Got a little side tracked," Tina replied.

Marilyn's ultra-sensitive nose twitched. "Really? How many times were you able to manage between waking and being here?"

"Umm...three and a half." Tina ripped off the plastic sheathing from around the freshly dry cleaned dress she was wearing. "What about you?"

"Twice," Marilyn said between applications of mascara. "Once on the vanity...the other, in the shower."

"The shower was our 'half.' Shampoo got in his eye...ruined the mood."

Marilyn giggled. Talking about their sex-capades relieved the tension of Marilyn's big day.

It was just the two of them. Best friends since before high school helping each other dress like they had for prom. Marilyn zipped up Tina's gossamer dress of sapphire blue, and Tina helped Marilyn with the sheath style white gown sprinkled with pearls and diamonds.

"Oh, Mike sent this over from Draylon for you to wear,"

Tina said, handing her a box.

"What is it?"

"I don't know. Hopefully not a rodent like he gave you last time."

"It was to be part of our meal in our wolf forms that night."

"Yeah well, leave me out of your 'nightly' rituals."

Marilyn opened the box to find a gold band of the Ouroboros and the Dacian emblem symbol combined. The dragon's eyes were encrusted with rubies and the wolf's eyes were emeralds. A note inside told her it was the crown worn by all the maidens given in marriage to their Zmei mates. Aiden Vamier had held onto it when he'd destroyed the Zmei clan. It now belonged to her to create a new beginning.

"Oh my God, it is gorgeous!" Marilyn breathed.

"May I place your crown on the 'fair maidens head'?" Tina offered then stopped. "Wait! I almost forgot...the veil."

A sheer webbing of diamond dusted material floated over her head and face. Tina adjusted it before carefully placing the ancient diadem of the Zmei onto her head.

A rapid knock sounded on the door. Marilyn's mother, Diane Reddlin peeked around. "How's it going? Are you two ready? There is an antsy Zmeu standing in the chapel about ready to go ballistic..."

"Tell him if he hadn't taken so long in the shower, I'd have been ready in time." Marilyn huffed.

Tina snickered behind her hand as she guided Marilyn towards the door, holding her train and end of her veil.

"You look beautiful, baby girl." Marilyn's mother raised the front of the veil and kissed her nose. "Didn't want to mess up the lipstick." She started to lead them out into the empty hallway towards the inner Dacian chapel but stopped abruptly. "Are you sure you want to marry a shape-shifter? I can get you hooked up with a nice young man who is a corporate executive in Manhattan."

"Thanks Mom, but no. Draylon is my destiny and I love him."

Her mother sighed and began walking again."What about you, Tina?" she asked again. "Harvey is a very nice young man, lots of potential...good provider..."

They stepped into the chapel as the Bridal March played and hundreds of Dacians and Vamiers stood to view their Zmei queen, the new generation of Dacia's Guardians. Down the long, carpeted aisle two men waited patiently. A dark-haired shape-shifting Dacian legend and a glowing aura of eternal light surrounding a Vietnam Veteran.

Tina shook her head. "Sorry Momma D, I don't think I could date a 'very nice young man'—I like them wounded and rough around the edges."

Rick Delvante stepped forward, offering his arm to his daughter as they took a step in time with the music moving them towards the future.

Fluffing both train and veil like a great bedsheet behind her best friend, Tina waited for her walk down the aisle. The best was yet to come. She'd recently received notice that the United

States Naval Academy Chapel would be available for a December wedding for two Immortal Angels.

Coming Late Summer 2015

<u>**Immortal Silence**</u>

ACKNOWLEDGMENTS

There are always those who go the extra mile when it comes to writing a novel. There are so many people to thank that I know I am going to forget some.

To my writing groups: **Maryland Romance Writers, Romance Writers of America, RomVets, Washington Romance Writers**—thank you for pointing me in the right directions.

To my critique group, the **Crit Divas and Devo**: *Amy, Teresa, Andy and Rena*—thank you all for putting up with me.

To the wonderful **Gladys of NerdGirlOfficial**—love you *Baby Bear* for all you've done to help me since we've met. My friends at **HallowRead** for your support.

For the great family of **Spiridus House**—welcome home. You all are the greatest!

To my "manager,"**Robert Carusone** who takes care of things so I can write. Thank you for taking on the task.

A book is never ready for the public until you have two things to go with it. One—a fantastic editor. **Judy Roth**, I would be just words on a page without your guidance. And two—a fabulous cover artist. **Jenji**, your artwork inspires me. You know exactly what I need.

To my family, both in-laws and out-laws, my wonderful brothers and sisters, both blood and bonded, thank you for your continued support.

To my daughters, you are inspiration and guidance…I am so proud of the young women you've both become.

And my husband…for being accepting of it all. I love you.

AUTHOR BIO AND LINKS

Born in north-central Michigan, Loni Lynne still loves the quiet woods, lakes and rivers in Otsego County and the Victorian era bay side houses of Little Traverse Bay. But after decades of moving around the country as a child and twenty-five years of marriage to her personal hero, she calls western Maryland her home.

Serving in the United States Navy didn't prepare her for the hardest job ever, being a stay at home mom, to her two wonderful daughters. After years of volunteering as a scout leader, PTA officer, and various other volunteer positions, all while still writing snippets of story ideas, her husband decided it was time for her to put her heart into *finishing* a story. He gave her a laptop, portable hard drive and his blessings to have a finished manuscript, ready to be sent out to the masses in one year. He created a writing monster.

LONI LYNNE HANGS OUT AT THESE PLACES:

Facebook Page for The Guardians of Dacia series: https://www.facebook.com/TheGuardiansofDacia

Loni Lynne's website: http://www.lonilynne.com

Loni Lynne's Facebook Page:https://www.facebook.com/lonilynne

Loni Lynne's Twitter Page:https://twitter.com/LoniLynne1

Loni Lynne's Goodread Page: https://www.goodreads.com/author/show/7115619.Loni_Lynne

Spiridus House–*A place where authors and industry specialists connect.* http://www.spiridushouse.com

Want to receive updates on future novels in *The Guardians of Dacia* series? Sign up for my newsletters at http://www.lonilynne.com/mailing-list.html

Want to make an author's day? Please let herknow by leaving a review on the site in which you bought herbook. Thank you! Remember...**read, review, repeat.**

Made in the USA
Charleston, SC
31 August 2015